THREE, IMPERFECT NUMBER

Patrizia Rinaldi

THREE, IMPERFECT NUMBER

*Translated from the Italian
by Antony Shugaar*

Europa
editions

Europa Editions
214 West 29th Street
New York, N.Y. 10001
www.europaeditions.com
info@europaeditions.com

This book is a work of fiction. Any references to historical events,
real people, or real locales are used fictitiously.

Library of Congress Cataloging in Publication Data is available
ISBN 978-1-60945-124-0

Rinaldi, Patrizia
Three, Imperfect Number

Book design by Emanuele Ragnisco
www.mekkanografici.com

Cover photo © Alexander Korobov/iStock

Prepress by Grafica Punto Print – Rome

Printed in the USA

Dedicated to Giulia and Maurizio,
and to their words:
Begin. Go on.

It's such a simple thing to make love.
It's like being thirsty and drinking.
Nothing could be simpler than being thirsty and drinking;
quenching one's thirst, feeling satisfaction at having done so;
no longer feeling thirst. Utterly simple.
—LEONARDO SCIASCIA, *One Way or Another*

THREE, IMPERFECT NUMBER

ennaro Mangiavento, stage name Jerry Vialdi, pulls past a line of tour buses along the Via Guglielmo Marconi. He parks his S.S.C. Napoli-sky-blue Fiat 500 and blesses it for its compact size:

At last, I can do without the Porsche Carrera. Now I'm finally my true self.

He looks at the people who have just stepped off the tour buses. The women are dressed in evening gowns at five o'clock in the afternoon, sequins glittering against sweat-sodden makeup.

Look at these rubes, here already. They can write articles about me in the *New York Times*, but the real money still comes from the usual crowd of ragtag losers. I flew all the way down to South America to bring back Sanjoval, with trumpet and all, but has it done me a bit of good? I promoted that minimal pussycat to the rank of poet with the aid of my beautiful voice and piano, and has it done me a bit of good? I've had women, men, and money by the shovelful, but has it done me a bit of good?

Vialdi sits in his car and remembers.

Right here is where I picked and chose among the rejected lyricists, because they treat me with respect inside the RAI building; they have no choice but to put on their smiles, and Zampani lets me use his studio which by now is practically mine, since he's never there. When they came to see me to be hired, they'd say: I'm Antonio D'Antonio and I'm a writer. I'm Mario Coppola and I'm an experimental author. I'm Ferdinando

Colasunto and I'm a poet. I always only had one answer: I'm Jerry Vialdi and I've got bad news for you: before I count to five you'd better be the fuck out of here. What the hell! Then the minimal pussycat, Gatta Mignon, showed up, a name I came up with personally, and short and rickety as she was, she opened her mouth and started to speak. She didn't say I'm a poet, I'm a writer, I'm experimentally good at this or that, instead she said, "You are the voice that stirs desire." That's what she said. And I took her on, because as far as ugly goes, she was ugly, but once she started talking I forgot all about that; if I could forget the fact while I was looking right at her, then Pussycat Mignon, without her face before them, could have satiated vast populations with her words. We'd sell them like hotcakes. The exact opposite of Rosina, who decided she was done with me last year, the fool. If Rosina wants to maintain her credibility, what she has to do is keep her mouth shut tight: short red hair she has, a flaming brushfire that only needs to be kindled, along with first-class thighs and neck. I didn't want to take her on at first because I used to go out on the town and run after women with her husband; I knew him well and it seemed wrong somehow. But then Rosina got my blood pumping and I decided to hire her anyway, because if there's one thing I like it's when one of God's creatures can go head-to-head with me, or lose their heads entirely. Rosina never stopped hating me, which is always worth something: when she meets me now her eyes light up, even worse than that brushfire, and one of these days she's going to run me down with the car I gave her. Mara, the pharmacist, represents a completely different level of danger, a far more ferocious one. Sometimes I make a date with her and then stand her up: frankly, Mara's thighs and legs frighten me, inside her stockings she carries a violent madness. She's particularly good at the work she does. One night, she saved me from an attack of vertigo. I called her and she came, and when I saw her standing there with the hypodermic needle in one hand, I thought to myself: here we go, this is the part where she kills me. Instead, she healed me. Not Julia, she's a flower, a blossoming rose, a delicate jasmine bud in full season. Of course, there's some tarnish on her bloom, because she's seen more than a few seasons in her time. She never makes high-handed demands, she's happy to take what we are for what we are; she's a different breed of woman, she's held onto her soul. I don't know how she's done it. I couldn't say, but perhaps she alone can conjure my soul back into existence. In any case, the most womanly of them all is still Gigi, and when he gets his claws into me he never lets me go, he's never even heard of the word soul or anything remotely resembling it. When he came into this world all he brought with him was his flesh; the spirit of the world beyond is something they clipped away along with his umbilical cord. He's a stunningly handsome devil. Forget about brushfires, he's got an eternal flame burning inside his chest. He's an advocate of pure evil and bad weather, his mouth spews gold and sea salt.

Vialdi gets out of the car. The flashing headlights tell him that the antitheft system is doing its job.

A woman in her fifties with rhinestone-studded shoes walks up to him.

"You're so good-looking, Jerry, you want to sign my record?"

"What do you have here, Signora? Did you dismantle the brakes on that bus?"

"What a charmer you are. You just have to make the dedication out to Annina." You have to do this, you have to do that. Jerry Vialdi's whole life has been a race to escape from *what you have to* and *what I tell you to*, and still they catch up with him. Almost invariably.

"I don't do dedications."

Before turning to enter the RAI building in Fuorigrotta, the ex-wedding singer and, later in his career, ex-neomelodic pop singer and, later still, ex-folk and traditional singer, and even later still ex-Ariston singer, then ex-star of musicals, until he finally became a sensitive singer winning the acclaim of the most discerning critics, turns and speaks to the looming horizon of the Polytechnic:

"If I'm ever reborn, I'm going to become an engineer and to hell with music and these ragtag losers in evening dress."

At the front door, the security guard doesn't bother asking for his pass, asking instead for predictions on the championship match.

"How's it going to go, boss?"

"This year is the *year*, brother, but we can't say it and we can't even think it because it'll bring terrible luck."

Jerry Vialdi leaves nothing to improvisation; he even rehearses his smiles in front of the mirror. In his dressing room he checks his image; he twists his head to one side, swings one hand up to cover his chest, spreads his fingers wide and presses them against his sternum, then smiles:

"You are," pause, "you are all my own warm heart of love."

The concert is a success; the sole annoyance is the excessive applause, distinctly not to his liking: he wants to include a few of the better numbers in his next live album. Well, they have technicians to take care of that.

In spite of all the depth of his musical erudition, he inevitably hits the high point of the evening with the same song: a crass little ditty featuring words of furtive sex in a car and the subsequent return home to his cuckolded wife. The phrase *Tu, solo tu, sei tu—you, only you, it's you*—of the refrain is the song's earworm.

A bona fide piece of crap. What came over Pussycat Mignon when she wrote it? Who can say? But I surely never thought she could serve up such a generous helping of tripe!

She turned in the lyrics four years ago. Let's set it to some fast-paced tune, loaded with percussion and *blam-blam* guitar riffs, she said. I objected, it's just too gruesome, I told her. You'll make enough money to buy a penthouse with another penthouse on top of it, she told me. And she was right. When I moved into the double-decker penthouse in Pozzuoli with a view of the water I nailed platinum honors to the walls, tributes to an awful song and a fraudulent confection of percussion and *blam-blam* guitar riffs. And as usual, the money came and quickly left. Money: it scampers off on quick little cat's feet, the elusive imp.

Jerry Vialdi strips off his basic black stage outfit and fine-tunes his street clothes of autumn-hued cashmere and corduroy trousers. The end of any concert still pumps him up to a boastful pitch and he channels it into a flood of beauty and rare courage.

He caresses his inside jacket pocket, whispers *for later* and drinks, with short sips, a foretaste of death.

1.

Detective Arcangelo Liguori was experiencing a moment of pure grace.

Even the sheer absence of minor defects forced him to admit how lucky he was. Even his fifty odd years, which were more odd than even, struck him once again as few and useful.

He told himself that perhaps it was all due to August in Sicily and in Ireland, the love affairs remembered and archived, the rediscovery of his body in a late-breaking recovery of various activities. Perhaps it was a reward for his ability to think quickly about situations that did not concern him and which therefore tickled his curiosity just enough. The void had filled up with lovely and chaotic dovetailing elements.

He was feeling good, and that made him dangerous, now that he could turn his improved mood to the pursuit he found most congenial: spoiling the good mood of everyone else around him, first and foremost among their ranks Captain Martusciello.

In October, his vitality hadn't diminished by so much as a fluid ounce and so, the minute he got back from the police station of Fuorigrotta, he strode into the administrative offices of Pozzuoli and went in search of Martusciello.

Captain Vincenzo Martusciello had spent what little summer vacation police regulations afforded him at a cut-rate holiday resort, with his wife Santina, his daughter Giulia, and his granddaughter.

Him, of all people—a man who refused to set foot on

Procida in August for fear of succumbing to his phobia of crowds—had sunk to the level of bartering his family's dignity for a miniclub. Upon contact with the place, the children had shown no obvious signs of fatal pathologies. Though it wasn't clear why.

At the discount beach club, the sea was like a vast plain, the sand belonged to lands that had never seen rain. The local sunshine had killed off any breezes and stowed them away in the dreary ice-cream receptacles.

After a while, Martusciello stopped thinking of himself as a husband, a father, and a grandfather, and had gained a new respect for certain land animals that were capable of reproducing without seeing the need to stick around afterwards.

The line for the swings had given him an indelible sense of melancholy and an uncomfortable realization: expectations for the future were deader than the stillborn breezes.

During the time he spent at the enchanting Ghiglia Resort, which he mentally referred to as Fanghiglia Resort—Bubbling Ooze Resort—he had half-persuaded himself that at least getting back to work would be a pleasure. He even expected to enjoy the morning commute on the ancient subway line, a term that was laughably applied to junkable train cars running on creaky old tracks.

But that's not the way it went.

The sticky brine of melancholy and relentless boredom had remained stuck to his heart, under his feet, and in the usual stab of pain on the right side of his body.

Upon his return, another inconvenience was joined to the long list of tiresome issues. The police captain found himself spending a week in the Ultramarine medical clinic, covered by his health plan, for the removal of a bodily appendage that he preferred not to discuss.

Laziness had been October's response. Walking the streets

until he was ankle-deep in them no longer warmed his heart. He felt no interest in human beings, animals, the streetscapes of alleys, lanes, and piazzas, that reasoning of emotion and logic that had always induced him to undertake depositions and interrogations with the eagerness of a marathon runner.

Indignation had gone to ground and, with it, the desire to stage and restage the experience of life, like a stubborn village mule that only follows the route that it knows and yearns for, however unfashionable it may be.

His wife Santina, who was visibly rejuvenating for reasons unknown, gazed at him with a consummate love that plucked at his nerves.

"So tonight, again, you're not working, you're not going out?"

"I'm not going out."

"Why not?"

"You've tormented me for most of a healthy lifetime with your *why aren't you staying in*'s and now you're starting on me with *why aren't you going out*'s?"

"Do as you like."

As you like. Sure. There was nothing he liked, there was nothing that interested him. He just wanted to step out of the line for the swings.

Liguori made his way to Martusciello's office by a roundabout route through a series of corridors, in order to avoid running into Deputy Peppino Carità, who had informed one and all that he preferred to be addressed as Giuseppe Càrita—literally and precisely, with the accent weirdly on the first *a* instead of the last. This new development seemed to date back to the diction and acting course that he had taken recently.

Martusciello pretended to talk into the Bakelite telephone that had accompanied him in his migrations from one office to another.

Liguori made himself comfortable and conveyed, with hand

gestures, that he really wasn't in a hurry. Then he gave the police captain one of his goofy half-smiles, which reckoned up the sum of annoyance added to mockery.

Martusciello jutted his chin in the direction of the telephone and waved his free hand in the air to say *this may go on for some time*. The detective spread out the other half of his smile to say *I'm in no hurry*, and then went over to the window and stood, looking out.

Even though it was nearly noon, the colors hadn't yet merged into the hot haze of muggy sunlight. The sea lay there, crystal clear, the tiny waves sweeping in toward the waterfront, topped with foamy white crests. Even at this distance, the dark blue was still blue, the white was still white. The ferry boats to the various islands boarded a few scattered foreign tourists. Liguori surveyed the improvised seamen's uniforms. He ran one hand over his linen shirt before sliding it into the pocket of his duck trousers, artfully wrinkled as they descended to meet the tops of his expensive leather shoes, which had cost as much as half of Giuseppe Càrita's monthly pay.

Martusciello broke off his phone conversation with a nonexistent colleague.

"Ah, gallant cavalier, a pleasure to see you!"

"Oh, it's been such a long time since I've been addressed by one of my rightful titles!"

Martusciello called Liguori cavalier, squire, proprietor of vast property, gentleman and scholar, prince, professor, count, and any other number of titles evocative of rank and learning. He liked to emphasize the fact that the detective had chosen to go into policework for his own amusement, not out of economic necessity or class affiliation.

Liguori's family had been members of the Neapolitan aristocracy for long centuries of sobriety and prestige, and Captain Martusciello spotlighted the sharp difference from his own birth by dragging out his *s*'s and putting on working-class dialect and aspirations.

"What now?"

"Someone's been murdered, Vialdi, the singer."

"*'O ssaccio*. I know. What do you want me to do about it?"

"Captain, what do you mean, what do I want you to do about it? Did you get a new job and forget to tell me?"

"Unfortunately, I didn't, but the Vialdi headache belongs to Captain Malanò and his Fuorigrotta office. And you just wait and see, that case isn't going to be just his for long, because Vialdi and the way they found his body is going to prompt a general outbreak of rubbernecking. The same itch you're here scratching right now."

Deputy Peppino Carità, alias Giuseppe Càrita, walked into the office with a tray and a demitasse cup.

Martusciello gave every sign of dismay.

Carità ignored him, continuing to stride toward the desk in a contrived posture, every muscle straining to make him look taller.

Liguori laughed.

"Are you wearing elevator shoes? Lift your pants leg, let me see."

The deputy froze to attention.

"No elevator shoes, sir."

"Sir?" Martusciello walked toward him, took the tray out of his hands, and set it down on his desk. "Peppino, ever since you've started doing amateur theater, you've gone soft in the head. And why have you stopped making coffee yourself? Why do you order in from the bar?"

"Giuseppe, if you don't mind. There's no regulation currently in force requiring me to make coffee."

Martusciello halted his arm, balancing the coffee cup halfway to his lips.

"In force requiring? Do me a favor, Peppino, get the hell out of here."

The deputy bowed from the waist, turned, and left. Martusciello glanced at Liguori:

"Aren't you going with him?" The detective shook his head and raised an eyebrow. "Pity."

"Now then, Martusciello, Captain Malanò wants our collaboration, Vialdi had been living in Pozzuoli for the past few years. You're not going to answer me? Fine, that just means I'll draft a report for you on my meeting with Captain Malanò."

"Excellent, do just that. And draft it in duplicate, so I can make sure to ignore both copies."

2.

Police Sergeant Blanca Occhiuzzi removed one of the earbuds that were driving Mozart right into the furthest corner of her brain.

She'd detected, in spite of the Mozart, a commotion out in the street, excessive even considering it was rush hour.

She lived in Fuorigrotta, across from the San Paolo Stadium, and she was accustomed to the sound of voices and cars, but that morning the noises outside indicated something out of the ordinary. She pulled the other earbud out of her other ear.

She made her way out to her balcony, and to her eyes the daylight was transformed into nothing more than a brighter shadow. She touched the railing, felt the warm metal. She leaned over.

She was on vacation, and she'd worked all summer long. In August Nini, her foster daughter, had left for London: fifteen years old and this was her first trip alone. Blanca had lost all appetite for vacation and solved a couple of cases instead.

She'd urged Nini to go, and now she was working overtime to compensate for eyes that knew only partial darkness. It wasn't reasonable.

The first night Nini was away, the sergeant went to sniff her pillow, the wisteria scent of Nini. The surviving senses had sharpened, and Blanca dominated the jurisdictions of sound, smell, and touch. She'd lost most of her sight and a great deal more in a fire when she was thirteen.

She sniffed at Nini's pillow. Then she promised herself that she wouldn't do it again.

"You and I have both lost too much already. There's no need to keep you from seeing everything you deserve to see, just so I can have a part of it."

The sergeant took advantage of Nini's absence to seek an assistant, something she'd never wanted before. She came to an agreement with Sergio Manzione, a twenty-something student from out of town. She'd chosen him for his irreverent manners; far better that than the usual unctuous pathos. She bought a compact car and began preparing to loosen her ties with Nini, at least in part.

The sounds from the street grew louder: sirens and screeching brakes and slamming car doors. From below the smell of gasoline and burning wafted up to her, gusts of the odor of frying mixed with the scent of rotting food. Blanca raised the sleeve of her sweater to cover the smell, then picked up the telephone, counted until she got to the speed dial button.

"Sergio, what's happening?"

"What do I know? I was asleep. Why don't you ask Nini?"

"Nini's at school. But don't you ever do any studying?"

"Don't even say it, Auntie, I ask myself the same thing all the time."

"Don't call me Auntie."

"Then you stop thinking about my failures in higher education. After all, what good's a degree in classical literature? Sheesh."

"Of course, they tied you up and blindfolded you when it was time to pick your major."

"What can I do for you, Blanca?"

"Come on by here, I have to go downstairs to see what's going on."

Sergio knocked on the door fifteen minutes later. Blanca

ignored the arm that the young man offered her and they headed down the stairs.

The woman walked with soft footsteps. Her body seemed to sense obstacles before brushing against or past them. Blanca's beauty lay not in the individual parts, but in the composition of contrasts. Her voice was younger than she was. Her short hair emphasized the femininity of her features. The beautiful sensuous lips protected irregular, slightly protruding incisors; when they opened into a smile it was unclear whether they were offering a bite or a kiss.

"Stay close to me but don't touch me. I'll reach out for you."

"Ah, if they could only hear you now, Auntie!"

"Shut up. You make me nostalgic for my dog."

"And I love you too."

The two of them were out on the street. Sergio explained to Blanca that there were policemen everywhere and crowds of people.

The sergeant tilted her head back.

"They're saying that someone killed Jerry Vialdi, the singer. They found the dead body between one set of goalposts of the San Paolo Stadium. Take me to a policeman, but pick me one who looks intelligent."

"How on earth did you manage to pick all that out with all this hubbub?"

"I can read lips."

"Touché."

After talking with a detective from the Fuorigrotta police station, Blanca Occhiuzzi asked Sergio to take her to her office in Pozzuoli:

"Summer vacation is over."

Blanca said goodbye to Sergio and reminded him of when she would be ready to go home.

The sergeant waited for the car to drive away.

She wanted to be left alone. She told herself that she was paying for Nini's new independence with pieces of her own. She concluded *it's worth it*: that girl was a daughter to her, more of a daughter than any child delivered in the blood of prayers and curses.

She stunned herself with the salt waves and the tufa-stone coast of the old harbor.

She needed freedom before seeing Liguori again. They hadn't seen each other in the past thirty-seven days. The precise accounting was not merely a matter of adding up the length of their respective vacation days.

The detective had called his colleague twice during the month of August: *I'm in Sicily*, *I'm in Ireland*, and not much more. Blanca had smiled at that need for geographic coordinates and had settled in to wait. Liguori unsettled her, made her feel like leaving and staying. She sensed the danger of his voice: it penetrated into the furthest corners of her brain, almost like the music of Mozart.

The sergeant was a specialist at decoding sounds and intentions in wiretaps and environmental listening devices. She'd trained in Belgium; she'd had excellent teachers, nearly all of them sightless, and a natural predisposition for which she was in great demand.

It wasn't part of her occupational baggage that allowed her to recognize in Liguori's voice hesitation, elegance, refined sensuality, and a devastating blend of derision and gentleness from which she would be well advised to turn and flee.

Before walking through the main entrance she took a deep breath, straightened her summer dress, and briskly swung ankles and flat sandals. She couldn't wear heels, she needed to sense the difference between pebbles and pavement.

Giuseppe Càrita, as all his colleagues, with the exception of Martusciello, were now resigned to addressing him, met her in the lobby:

"*Sergeant,*" he intoned. He had been taking elocution lessons for some time. "You're looking particularly magnificent today."

"Thanks, Giuseppe, how are your theatrical studies coming along?"

"Blanca, with you I can talk the way it comes naturally to me, I've found my own personal paradise. How wonderful it is to become different people: kings, lawyers, peasants, sons of bitches, Garibaldi, and Aisauer."

"Who?"

"'Under the cloud of threatening war, it is humanity hanging from a cross of iron.' Those are his words."

"Ah, Eisenhower. You're performing Eisenhower?"

"We're studying him in the auto repair shop where we rehearse. Our maestro . . . you understand who the maestro is, don't you? He's the actor who does the commercial for OraPerOra, the diet pill."

"I can't seem to recall."

"Odd that you can't seem to recall, because he's famous. Anyway, our maestro takes pieces written and spoken by famous figures from history, blends them together in a phenomenal collage that only he could create, and has us recite them on Saturday evenings in front of relatives."

"His relatives?"

"No, ours. Modestly speaking, I help to bulk up the audience because I have two . . . I have a large family. The maestro even offers me a discount, and lets me pay five euros instead of seven for the group ticket."

"Generous of him."

"I couldn't say if it's generous, because I already pay for the course, but True Art isn't cheap, as you know. And enjoying multiple lives is priceless."

Blanca had to agree.

She climbed to the floor where the captain's office was located. The police officers moved silently and encouraged visitors to cause as little noise as possible. They explained to her that Martusciello had come back from his vacation with a dead-tired face and had announced that for the next few months he was going to lead a solitary life in the office.

Blanca was only slightly concerned, if at all. With her, Martusciello exhibited manners that he wouldn't concede to other, lesser individuals.

She headed toward his office, expecting the faint scent of tobacco, salt air, sulphur, and the aroma of second-rate shaving cream.

She walked past a window. She didn't see the shop fronts, the strolling pedestrians, three cats stretched out in the sunlight. She didn't see the ship, in the nearby dry dock, offering the gaping mouth of its broken front hatch. She didn't notice the women walking arm-in-arm with the last traces of summer.

But she did sense the stirrings of life, down by the waterfront.

They'll have found you first thing in the morning. I even know who'll have been the first to spot you, that idiot who reeks of wine and eternal clothing.

He'll have turned on every spotlight on the field just for the fun of defacing the dawn. Good work, that means he wallowed in the flood of light in the middle of the spectacle. It's not something you see every day, scoring a goal with a dead body.

Much less yours.

A famous dead body.

The hammock netting will cradle the perpetual slumber of your renowned body. How poetic.

Makes you want to lick your whiskers.

I prepared you beautifully for the show, as per orders received: I set you up in a fetal position, you always used to say that living is already dying a little bit, what a mediocre thought. And after all, you were always such a little baby boy! So I equipped your banality and even delivered you a tidbit, a mouthful of meadow in your mouth. Suckle nicely on your grass nipple. Console yourself for eternity.

The drunkard and his stench will have approached the goalposts closest to the cemetery, I picked them special.

Whoever looks at you has already been infected.

The idiot will certainly be incapable of appreciating the refinement of the thing.

You see all the gifts I give you? Come, give us a peck on the cheek, don't be shy! Hug me, call me your little man, kid brother, *sister, old friend. You're so fond of rummaging through family names for strangers you never see, that you forget about even as you're watching them.*

Say it to me: genius, angel, friend, dear heart, mother love. Recite once again the rosary of slimy flattery.

Whore. Worm. Scabby wound, sewer of my hatred.

Slap your tongue against your palate to give birth to sounds, songs, grunts of advanced passion. Of friendship that you don't even know. Of eternity that is beneath your consideration. Of filthy, disgusting beauty.

The lives and lives that you tear asunder.

You turned me into a man who'd been castrated with all his senses wide awake. You turned me into a woman who'd given birth to her own demise. A beast, drawn and quartered. Vertebrae dangling from the meat hook of your ill will.

It's dull, you know, not to have a face.

It's difficult to insist with this stump, to go on being alive.

You no longer have this problem. Maybe right now you're the riveting star of the autopsy session, perhaps the conscientious doctor is plunging in the scalpel as I speak, and it's just too bad that you can't feel the sweetness of the slice.

Good night, brother.

5.

Blanca walked into Martusciello's office and found him there with his hands crossed over his stomach, his head lolling back against the upper edge of his backrest, and his eyes shut.

The captain only noticed that she was there when it was already too late. He snapped into a more decorous position. Blanca made him feel more awkward than he usually did, and always had, from the first time they met. He could feel parts of his body drifting out of place, into disjointed poses and gestures. His movements all went wrong in the presence of a woman who made it clear that she perceived the space around her in a clearly mastered equilibrium.

"Weren't you on vacation?"

"I was. Then I heard that they found Jerry Vialdi's dead body at the San Paolo Stadium, in a fetal position, jammed into a corner of the goalpost net. He had a blade of grass clenched between his teeth. It seemed like an excellent reason to come back."

"I have no wish to pursue the case, nor do I want you to do so. I can already imagine the horde of idiots and prurient rubberneckers that this murder is bound to attract. Plus I don't want to hear Liguori's voice in my ears with his theories, I don't want to be exhausted by his frenzy for coming and going, I just can't take it. I've had a trying summer."

"I heard that you had an operation . . . "

"Why doesn't he get cancer of the tongue? I had an operation and I don't want to talk about it." He lowered his voice to a whisper: "Anyway, that's not the reason."

"Not the reason for what?"

"I'd forgotten that you can hear a flea cough!"

Martusciello told her the tale of the misbegotten summer that refused to go away. He told her about indelible objects: the swing with its insatiable creaking noise; the restaurant's neon lights fully lit even though sunset had scarcely begun; sandals on the beachfront with the arid sand, back and forth in an Olympian boredom; the rough sheets that had certainly enjoyed a previous existence as raincoats; the ice cream in the refrigerated vaults.

Blanca smiled, drew close to the police captain and planted two kisses on his cheeks, cheeks that were bristly and did not smell of second-rate shaving cream.

They were still standing there cheek to cheek when Liguori came in.

"Ah, there you both are! Captain, what's up, are you all better? Blanca, you have curative powers, you're better than an ointment for . . . "

"I always ask myself and I never find an answer," Martusciello hastened to interrupt him. "But why should a citizen, the proprietor of vast properties, with a vast array of books that tell him this, that, and the other thing, a squire without a horse, but with heaps and heaps of cash that could suckle him on crates of wine, why should such an individual land right at my feet? Why, oh why? If you'd decided to be a scientist, if you'd listened to mama and papa, we'd all have led much quieter lives. No, sir, because of that curdled brain of yours you decided to pursue your whim of becoming a policeman. A wealthy policeman. You tell me if such a thing should be."

While Martusciello went on talking, Liguori had set down his report in duplicate on the desktop, and had then stepped over beside Blanca and with a light touch of his hand to her back had guided her to a chair. Then he'd pulled up another chair, dragging it across the floor to interrupt the captain's speech and placing it next to the one where the woman was seated.

The detective's aroma reached Blanca: a blend of linen, leather, and traces of some feminine scent.

"How's everything, Liguori?"

"Just fine, thanks. No need to inquire after your well-being, you're paler and more beautiful than ever. Well, then, what do you say we talk about work? You know, just to remind ourselves of why they pay us a salary," he glanced over at Martusciello, "which, as you so rightly point out, I don't even need."

Martusciello returned the glance, with venom. Liguori maintained his composure.

"Malanò, the captain in Fuorigrotta, wants our assistance. He summoned me to his office to extend a formal request, he tells me that he can't reach you on the phone. Shameless liars! For the past several years, Vialdi had been living in a rooftop apartment and penthouse on the border between Bagnoli and Pozzuoli. Martusciello, think of the luck: his residence is the first one over the line. Vialdi's corpse was found—"

"We already know," Martusciello cut him off. Liguori shot him a half-smile and went on.

"It was found in the goalposts of the San Paolo Stadium, the goal closest to Fuorigrotta Cemetery. A groundsman with a weakness for alcohol made the happy discovery and waited only half an hour before calling the police. Apparently he remained poised in uncertainty as to whether the huddled corpse with the blade of grass in its mouth might not be an illusion conjured up by the glass he'd just downed. The autopsy results are not yet available. Last night, Vialdi played a concert at the RAI Auditorium in Via Marconi, and I went there in person: no interesting news emerged, the usual praise and proclamations in favor of the late singer. No unusual behavior had been observed. Captain Malanò believes that the bizarre funeral rites might have been the work of a serial killer."

Martusciello turned red in the face, lit a cigarette, and launched into a diatribe against the gendarme and his obsession with imaginary serial killers. He was incapable of logic. He was incapable of curiosity when it came to logic. Malanò had no reasonable relationship with statistics. He couldn't overcome the tedium of poring over bank accounts and telephone call records. He was incapable of pounding the streets, using good old shoe leather to canvas the neighborhood for information about the victim, asking even the walls. He lacked the subtle violence that could push interrogation sessions from the present to the *remote infinitive.*

At the words *remote infinitive* Blanca smiled, and in fact Liguori could not tolerate the poetic license.

"You, on the other hand, have a truly stunning understanding of the remote infinitive." He stretched out his legs. "A marriage between Kantian category and third grade textbooks."

"The marriage between your mother and father led to the birth of this masterpiece of applied science. Let it go, Liguori: relax."

"I'd like to, but what exactly are you smoking?"

"Fine, okay, let's do this: you can be fully in charge of the case of the serial killer, where the series for now is stationary at the number one. I will investigate from here the interesting life of the famous singer, and Blanca can give me a hand in my research and put up with Giuseppe Càrita."

"Agreed, as long as Blanca can give me a hand as well."

Blanca stood up to go into his office.

"Three is an imperfect number," she said.

6.

Rosina Mastriani did her best to be even tempered and sunny with Dottor Criscuolo at the employment office. She couldn't spare any more time. She wanted a yes or a no, and she wanted it immediately.

Rosina was in a hurry. After moving away from home, she'd been fired from the only job she'd been able to find, at the Call Center N.D. ("Insure Your Life and Life Will Smile Back"), because:

she hadn't obtained results;

she wasn't fast enough;

she wasn't alluring enough;

her voice wasn't loud enough to be heard;

she had once or twice broken into tears while talking with a potential client;

she never accommodated the psychological requirements of the potential client;

she was unable to explain the crucial importance of insuring the lives of others, much less her own, at a minimal level;

it was obvious from miles away that she wasn't enthusiastic about going all the way to San Giovanni a Teduccio every morning at seven and returning home with darkness in the sky and in her eyes;

and because she lacked optimism.

The Executive Leader, Technical Support, Mario Apicella, known to his underlings as "Stress 'em Out," in his rare moments of interpersonal interaction, wanted to be referred to as "The Boss." Mario Apicella was thoroughly familiar with the behavioral norms expected of the call center employees. The notification of redundancy was communicated by Dottor Apicella to Rosina with merciful rapidity, in a charming tone of voice, respectful of the psychological requirements of his interlocutor:

"Mastriani, you'll find a better position, wait and see. After all, the work you're doing is well below your educational level."

Rosina bit violently into the inside of her cheeks to keep from uttering the rapid sequence of words that her tongue was on the verge of spitting out.

After the exit interview she returned home and sat there, alone, racking her brains: there must be another opportunity out there somewhere, however hard it might be to find.

Equally difficult to find was her own automobile, which she had parked on the sidewalk. When she finally spotted it she realized that she had been parked in by two other cars. Immediately afterward she read a sign on her windshield warning her not to try to move her vehicle: the police had clapped a wheel clamp onto the car.

As soon as she climbed onto the bus she set out to count all the shades of gray and brown along the Via Marina. She took advantage of the opportunity as well to count all the months of rent that she could still afford to pay: three, tops, if she also stopped eating.

A very polite gentleman stood and offered her his seat. But it was just an excuse to rub up against her arm. So she waited patiently, stood up, smiled at the very polite gentleman, and pulled the cord for the next stop. The very polite gentleman eagerly accepted the implicit invitation, as well as the place in front of the door. As soon as the bus doors swung open, Rosina counted to three, coincidentally the number of months she could pay rent, and shoved him off the bus.

By the time the very polite gentleman got back to his feet with a curse, the doors had already closed. She blew him a kiss out the window.

"On days like this I learned that it's possible to murder someone, and you just chose the wrong day."

Then she thought about how they'd found Jerry Vialdi's corpse.

Ninety minutes later, she got back to her studio apartment in Pianura. She turned on her computer and put both car and wheel clamp up for sale.

"Jerry Vialdi, even now that you're dead, you continue to draw down curses on my already amply cursed existence. I can't afford to keep the car you gave me. The next one I buy is going to have a sunroof. Every time I look up I'll laugh loudly, right in your face."

She wondered who she could turn to for a job, where she could go, and what the hell remained for her to try now; she bit into an annurca apple and tried not to think about her kids, who didn't even want her anymore, and the memory of all that she no longer possessed.

She turned the apple-scented knife over and over in her hands and slowly cut into her knee.

"Signora . . . " Dottor Criscuolo was reading the CV, " . . . Signora Mastriani, you know, at your age it's hard to find a position. Your university degree is actually a hindrance. The slightest possibility of successful placement is . . . is . . . In any case, we'll let you know."

"But I know your exact placement. Right here." And Rosina Mastriani held her hand up against her throat.

Then she left the office, moving nicely. That was something she knew how to do. She considered the way in which she'd beaten someone to the termination point, the way she always seemed to do, whether it was with women or men. And she decided:

"Fine, that just means that if I can't find an easy job I'll have to get a hard one."

Mara Scacchi put on her lab coat roughly and awkwardly: a button flew under the eighteenth-century cabinet. She stretched out on the floor to reach the button.

That was how her father found her: as she was trying to stretch her arm out all the way to the wall.

"Mara, what are you doing?"

"I'm filling a prescription. What does it look like I'm doing?"

"Well, well, calm and courteous as always. Yesterday, when you were out God knows where, a couple of policemen dropped by to ask questions. They wanted to check our sales of psychopharmaceuticals in the last month. I'd have to guess it had something to do with the murder of your friend."

"He wasn't my friend, he was my lover."

"Thanks so much for setting me straight. Did you kill him?"

Mara Scacchi did her best to keep her implacable legs under control, though they were determined to go elsewhere.

Father and daughter looked at each other for a long time, in a silent duet of ancient resentments.

The warehouse man called the pharmacist to ask him for a pro forma invoice.

Mara blessed her rescuer, went to the bathroom, locking the door behind her, and put her wrists under cool running water for a while. Then she reached into her lab coat pocket and found a surrogate for the peace of mind she'd just lost.

7

During the break between classes, Nini switched on her phone. Ever since Blanca had hired Sergio to go places with her, the girl had kept her phone turned off during classtime. Before that, no; before that, despite the rule that no one followed anyway, she just kept the ringer muted and continually checked the display.

One time her high school teacher, Prof. Trisurname, officially registered with her employer as Professoressa Miniati Greco Valsassi, had even disqualified her classroom essay:

"Russo, what are you looking at under your desk? Bring me your classwork and your cell phone. Disqualified and confiscated, respectively."

Prof. Trisurname had no idea that every time Nini heard her last name, a ferocious rage surged up deep inside her, a rage that she'd learned to conceal.

Her father, Gianni Russo, was doing time in prison, for her mother's murder. Blanca had explained to the girl that her father was innocent: he'd been forced to confess. Orders from above. Nini replied that the word "innocent," applied to her father, just made her laugh. She'd failed to add that from the day her mother'd fallen in love with the son of the man who owned the factory where she worked, Gianni Russo had been killing her anyway, on a steady diet of fists and threats.

Nor did she remind Blanca that her father had kidnapped her and left her at a girlfriend's apartment, all the better to drive her mother insane. All this, when she was twelve years old.

Carmen, the factory worker who was one of her mother's close friends, had secretly gone to get the girl. She had secretly conveyed her to the sergeant's home.

There was no need to tell Blanca the things she already knew. She'd cracked the case herself, together with Martusciello and Liguori, she'd lost her service dog in the process, and she too had come frighteningly close to being killed.

Then finally the foster parenting request had been approved: Nini could live with Blanca by law.

The categories of DNA did not include their story of daughter mothers, non-mother mothers, young old women, old young women, desperate embraces in search of other embraces to replace those that had been lost.

There was plenty more that Prof. Trisurname failed to comprehend.

While her classmates crowded into the high school café, Nini was finally able to read Blanca's text message:

"I've gone back to work on an important case. On the top right shelf in the refrigerator there's an escarole pie."

Nini smiled: when Blanca told her where things were, she became very detailed and specific. As if the girl too had problems with her sight.

Sometimes the kind of phrases that emerged were: look out for the third step going up after the elevator, there's a section of marble tread toward the handrail that's wobbly. They've moved the bus stop ten steps over to improve access to that idiot's driveway.

For Nini, that precision in the enunciation of difficulties she'd never faced only became another rediscovered embrace.

The smile vanished from Nini's lips: Tita, the girl who sat next to her in class and had gone with her on their first summer trip, was weeping at the counter, in front of everyone.

Nini made her way through the crowd to Tita with some difficulty, took her by the arm, and led her outside:

"What's the matter?"

"Someone murdered Vialdi. My mother is in danger."

8

Captain Malanò climbed onto his Ducati Multistrada after checking carefully to make sure it was exactly as he had left it when he parked it. Intact.

At forty he still felt like a boy: studio apartment with a galley kitchen on Via Posillipo in the space that was once his father's ground floor concierge booth; a rapid climb upward through the ranks thanks to remarkable scholarly exploits integrated with, and actually carried out during, police operations; civil service exam passed successfully and on to the next thing; undergraduate degree achieved with the same techniques: studying at night, working by day, and vice versa.

Small daisy chains of discreet favors performed helped him along the road to, first, his degree, and afterward, the captainship of the Fuorigrotta police station.

Now life lay before him: he was *multistrada,* suitable for both paved and unpaved roads, just like his flame red Ducati; the serial killer case was sure to shorten his wait in the bureaucratic antechamber for the position of deputy police chief.

Here's what people had to say about him:

"Handsome and amiable, let no one deny it, easy on the eyes and easy to talk to. But don't you ever try to get between him and whatever stewpot he has his eyes on, because he'll tear you limb from limb, or have you torn limb from limb by someone he sends to do the job."

And here's what Malanò had to say about himself:

"My life begins at age forty." He liked nothing so much as

a trite cliché. "As a boy I studied and I helped my father, then I had to beef up my shoulders, bowed from years of studying, then I went on working and studying, and progressed from that to studying and working. All this after being orphaned of my mother at age six. Only one love in my life, a bastard woman who's still lodged firmly right here, in my heart." Malanò was no fan of sophisticated lyrics in music. "So much the better, it just means that all the other bastard women on the prowl will find that vacancy occupied. Now my life, finally, belongs to me."

He revved the bike and shot off toward the morgue. He meant to have a conversation with Dr. Grimaldi about the autopsy performed on the notorious corpse, which fate—well aware of the sacrifices he had made—had been so kind to lay on his doorstep. Fate, duly informed of the situation, had chosen one particular doorstep, smack in the heart of the soccer stadium where, in the earliest days of his career as a cop, choruses and choruses of soccer fans had hollered into his face *chi non salta celerino è, è!*—an old anti-cop soccer fight song.

Captain Malanò couldn't have explained how or why he was happy when he rode his motorcycle. Just, very simply, that he was happy.

The beltway gave him a turbocharged itch for speed, an itch he was all too happy to scratch, with gusto. He started singing Vialdi's biggest hit: *Tu, solo tu, sei tu. Sei il sole al mattino, la luna la sera. Tu, solo tu, sei tu. Il mio cuore sbagliato se ne va e poi ritorna. Perchéééé tu, solo tu, sei tu.* Because it's you, only you, just you.

Dr. Carmine Grimaldi welcomed Malanò like a thorn in the trachea.

There was nothing he liked about the man: not the unseasonal leather jacket, not the oversized motorcycle, not the bandanna, an even brighter red than the motorcycle, not the beefed up body with its bulging bands of muscle, not the swagger, not the hand that kept wandering back to the holstered pistol as if it were a woman's breast, reassuring simply because it had chosen him. Him and no one else but him.

He also didn't like the words the man used: they came out of Malanò's mouth with their party suits rumpled and torn. Those rips revealed threadbare, filthy linings.

Grimaldi's almost seventy years made him think that the police captain of Fuorigrotta had a long-term goal that was the fruit of irritating ambition and unremarkable intelligence.

"You're here," was his greeting. "I can tell you immediately that the results will take a while, we can't seem to establish the cause of death. From a quick initial glance I'd be inclined toward heart attack, but further investigation is called for. One thing is clear: the singer experienced sleep, followed by death."

"And that's it?"

"And that's it."

"Why can't you identify the cause of death?"

"Why do most murders go unsolved?"

"The same old story, Grimaldi. You say the same thing every murder they bring you, you're getting old."

The doctor looked down at his hands. He studied, as if they weren't his own, the spots, the wrinkles, the skin that folded over the clenched knuckles and the fragility that was consuming his fingernails.

"Right. Unless you have any other questions, I'll be going."

"Wait! Wait. Is it possible that the corpse was transported from the road to the stadium goalposts by a single person?"

"Anything's possible. I'll provide you with a full report on the facts, you all can have your fun with your theories."

"It's more than a theory. A dead body propped up on a soccer goalpost with grass stuffed in its mouth necessarily makes one think serial killer. Come on!"

"Ah, so you really like this idea of a serial killer: you're forgetting where we are, even killers need someone to issue a permit of residency. And you're not the office they turn to. Take good care of yourself, Malanò."

The captain returned to his red motorcycle and checked it before throwing his leg over the seat. He did it again. He did it every time.

9.

I didn't have a lot of options. Perhaps I was always pushing them away with my own hands. Who can say? Certainly not someone with my blood, someone who doesn't even know where the highborn blood has flowed to.

When I decided that my inadequacy in life could be something to brag about, a knife I could seize from the blade's end, I started to show off my memory and knowledge.

Lalalalà, I remember all the fragrances. The trifling offenses of rotten peaches and two-bit martyrdoms.

Lalalalà, the clothes I'm wearing are inadequate to the gigantic desire for revenge, so I buried them in a drawer.

Lalalalà, O you who still bear love for me, understand that I know it's only a love of injuries.

Lilililì, there's the sewer down which I pour all my knowledge.

Lilililì, on that lightless table I stripped books and learning of all their varnish, with the use of a blowtorch and a welder's mask.

Lilililì, in those hues I trilled like an eerie hoopoe and reeled off names to be remembered by those who, unlike me, will live on.

Lilililì, around the corner of the day before yesterday, I was the magister militum hiding under the bed.

Lilililì, on that other bed, I lost my identity and shape and now I'll never know if I'm a man, a woman, or both.

Not that killing ever put me in an especially good mood, but *at least it makes me feel I'm alive. It satiates me with flight, terror, hiding places, here's the noise of the people coming to get you. You know. Those kinds of things.*

All of them.

Except for guilt, I killed it too, in all the previous lalalalà's and lilililì's.

10.

Martusciello had almost reached the floor of his office when he changed his mind and headed back downstairs. At the front door the police officer asked him if he'd left something in his car.

"No," the captain said, spreading his arms, "I left everything in the subway."

He forced himself to walk. He didn't feel like it, but his abulia, which was already moving house inside his head, was bothering him. He decided that there had been other periods like this, but he'd never allowed the void to taint his life in that manner. Not even when his wife Santina left him and then came back as if nothing at all had happened.

He looked at his shoes, with the same old laces, the ones he'd been buying in the same shop for years:

"You don't feel like it? Well, you have to walk all the same."

He headed over toward the narrow lanes behind the port, from which there was no view of the water.

Without planning out his route, he found himself skirting the tracks of the Cumana railway, which had been sidelined forever until someone could reorganize and put it at the service of other rail lines. For the moment, the Cumana remained nothing more than a hustle and bustle of local trains, bedaubed with modern graffiti that was already ancient, flaking signs in fading hues.

A few glimpses of flowers that had survived the harsh stones and searing summer gave him respite from his abstraction.

The pain in his ankle, which served as a rudimentary pedometer, reminded him of the pleasure that had still been his to enjoy not even all that long ago: the enjoyment of long treks, the effort of slow intelligence, of going on just as long as he could and even then, a little longer. And he felt a solitary delight in the anyway and all the same.

For the first time in months he was brushed by a smooth consideration of good intentions.

He told himself that if he succeeded with the street, if he plunged into it to the point of taking pleasure from even the rocks and the rotten food and the filth, then he could try again with his work as well, with all the troubles at home and with his age that refused to stop advancing. It would turn into a sort of training.

I'll turn it into a daily exercise and I'll shatter with my many footsteps the void that insists on lodging in this head of mine.

Martusciello had built himself with simple and obstinate resources. He remembered all too clearly the derision, expressed in words and gestures, of his enterprising colleagues. He'd always been an ordinary beat cop, the kind who refused to corrupt whores of all kinds and levels of income, the kind who never swore, who didn't want to modernize, who went around town with his pistol unloaded, who had only ever had two options: a miserable end or the *Pubblica Sicurezza*— Naples's finest. He rejected proclamations, but as far as he was concerned, when it came to *Pubblica Sicurezza*, the only Safety really did rest in the hands of the Public.

Public, now, let's not go overboard, he thought. The job that I wanted, or maybe I should say, the job that wanted me, that landed on my shoulders because of how and where I was born, was to keep safe the little patch of territory that I could keep an eye on. A patch that wasn't for sale to the highest bidder, that was without newspaper advertising, and far from the realm of these two-bit sharks that come onto the market with their heads decapitated only to be replaced by a swordfish head. So they can be sold again, new and improved.

As he walked, Martusciello headed back toward the sea, along the boundary with the Bagnoli quarter. He found he had fetched up outside Jerry Vialdi's house.

He looked up and saw that from the recessed terraces of the two-story penthouse there extended a host of plants: a garish livery at a wedding ceremony between sea and sun. To rest his eyes from that incongruous splendor he turned them toward the islet of Nisida.

"You're even prettier in October," he said. "I can't think of anything better to say, it's an outright declaration of love."

Nisida was beautiful, and nothing more need be said. Set on the surface of the sea as if it were about to set sail any second, due to its inherent superiority over the horrors surrounding it, the island had remained uncontaminated over the years because it housed the Juvenile Correction Institute and, uncaring, flaunted its Mediterranean maquis, sea, and past.

Every so often some especially zealous politician would suggest turning it into a casino, a resort, a residential development, or a theme park.

In the meantime, the prison stood, preserving with its indifference the regret over what the Campi Flegrei could have been.

11.

Martusciello stepped closer to the row of buzzers by the front door, read the name "Maestro Jerry Vialdi," and rang. He expected no response, the gesture was just his way of trying to get closer to the case.

But a woman's melodious voice answered him:

"Who is it?"

The captain was surprised, especially because Vialdi was the only person listed as an occupant of the apartment.

"It's Police Captain Vincenzo Martusciello."

He walked to the door, took one look at the broken police seals, and knocked.

The woman who opened the door to him didn't match the voice that had responded on the intercom: age impossible to judge, short, skinny, shoulders wrapped around her own sternum.

Martusciello looked through the door to find the owner of that voice, then the woman spoke.

"I know that I've committed a crime."

Even the police seals fell back into place. It wasn't just a matter of the timbre: hesitation mixed with apparent calm that was, however, belied by imprudent *r* sounds whisked Martusciello to a soft comfortable place. That woman spoke with the sound of asbestos kisses.

The captain extended his hand with the awkward gesture of someone incapable of judging distances effectively and therefore obliged to lean forward from the waist.

"I'm Vincenzo Martusciello. Why did you ignore the police seals?"

"I'm Marialuigia Moreno." She smiled, and her green eyes darkened. "I wanted to water the plants."

"And you're willing to risk jail time to water the plants?"

"See for yourself."

Marialuigia Moreno led Martusciello onto the upstairs terrace, which was hidden from the street.

The captain admired the array of wisteria, bougainvillea, and miniature white climbing roses, and patches of meadow in broad low planters dotted with wild daisies.

She waved her hand.

"Two days, and they've all withered."

"You can't buy seedlings, you need to buy seeds. They should be planted in large planters with good soil for flowering plants. They need lots of water."

Martusciello walked over to the railing and leaned over: on the terrace below he made out the shapes of the plants that could be glimpsed from the street as well: palm trees, short powerful trunks exploding with excessive glee, saplings crowded into a cluster of vases from Vietri and the Benevento area.

The vegetation was all starting to wither, but it hardly struck Martusciello as much of a loss.

"What a difference, downstairs."

"Well, at least that's not my fault." The woman laughed and made music. "I selected the plants on the upper terrace and I take care of them, that's all. It's not my job: I wrote the lyrics for Jerry's songs, or at least I have been for the past several years. Modestly speaking, *Tu, solo tu, sei tu* is my work. You know it?"

"Everyone knows it! And with all my respect for your musical artistry, it's uglier than that wrought-iron bench over there."

"The previous album hadn't sold the way Jerry expected,

and so I brought that monstrosity into the world, and in fact it sold like hotcakes. *Tu, solo tu, sei tu* paid for the double-decker penthouse. Far too often my work has had no relationship to speak of with musical artistry."

"Talk to me about the victim."

"There were disagreements and arguments aplenty, but if you care about someone you wind up fighting with them, don't you? And Jerry was so generous with the people who worked for him. He put my life back on track."

"You have a very pretty voice."

Marialuigia Moreno pressed her hand against the pit of her stomach, took a few deep breaths, and then began to sing, even improving the health of the daisies.

When she was done singing the number from Jerry Vialdi's repertoire, she stood for a moment in silence.

"Yes, I know how to sing."

"Yes, you do know how to sing. Why don't you sing your own songs?"

"You need to have a soloist's physique, and I don't have it."

Martusciello and the woman walked back inside, and the captain took a look around.

"Care for something to drink, Captain?"

"I'd better not, I don't want to become an accomplice to your breaking and entering, even after the fact. Who hated Vialdi enough to murder him in that way?"

"I don't know. Not everyone loved him, of course. I'd venture a guess: his more talented and less successful rivals, perhaps, but I doubt that any of them would go so far as to commit murder."

"Did he frequent any questionable individuals, have any ties to organized crime?"

Marialuigia Moreno curled her legs beneath her on the sofa and turned into a cat.

"Jerry had some bad habits, but actual ties to organized

crime, no, I doubt it." She shut her mouth. "And if he had, I wouldn't tell you about it."

"That phrase could be taken as a confirmation."

"I don't know. Why would he have even told me about such a thing?"

"Because if you care about someone you wind up fighting with them and talking to them."

"I was an employee of his, and what friendship there was was a product of working together. That's all."

Martusciello understood that she was done confiding in him.

"Shall we go, Signora?"

"Sure, I don't have far to go, I live in a studio apartment in the other wing of the building. The one overlooking the tufa-stone, not the salt water." She cocked her head to one side. "Are you going to arrest me?"

"Let's not overdo things. You inspire trust in me. But, take it from me, forget about the plants."

"Can't I at least take a few of them away with me?"

"It wouldn't be a very smart move."

"Sure, for me or for them. They'd die in any case. Where I live there's not much light and no outdoor spaces. Let's go."

Martusciello did his best to put the seals back the way they were and headed toward the stairs.

"One last question: why didn't I see your name in the credits on Vialdi's CDs?"

"Because my byline is Gatta Mignon, a nom de plume that he came up with for me. I won't be using it again, and I won't be writing any more songs either."

12.

On the way back, being tenaciously loyal to annoyance, Martusciello could not bring himself to admit that he'd glimpsed anything worthy of curiosity. What he felt was a defective desire to know more, but still, the desire had finally come to him.

He almost dismissed it:

"Nothing much."

He mused: A woman, not pretty, an unsuccessful soloist, who then looks around for a job of some kind, at a certain point finds herself writing lyrics for a singer who also isn't much but who still manages to sell a substantial number of records. No doubt, Marialuigia is obliged to keep her face calm and her emotions under control, in the midst of the benefits that have rained down on her so unexpectedly. Short enough to drown in one of the puddles of that rainstorm of good luck, actually. Marialuigia Moreno seems to be missing certain parts of a normal sized body. But what a voice she has. So lovely. This Jerry must have sucked the art right out of her, with the permission of Gatta Mignon herself, after all she wanted nothing better than a chance to go buy herself some plants. She inspires trust in me, she strikes me as a creature with her feet on the ground. One who was perfectly aware that the fancy silverware never actually belonged to her, but who also understood clearly that if things had gone differently, she never would have even heard the silverware clank with a ringing sound as she washed up and put it away into the silverware drawer. Which also didn't belong to her. She looks like an prematurely old girl doing everything she can to justify the second-rate world that surrounds her, but goes on devouring it all the same, even finding it tasty and nourishing from time to time. Hummphh. She made quite an impression on me, no doubt. Yes, a little something of an urge to dig into her life and the life of the Singing Maestro did start to stir inside of me, not much, just a little. I did like the fact that she was reluctant to empty the bucket of lifelong sins over the head of the dearly departed. She didn't drip out a teary rendition of *oh how I loved and will always miss my lord and master.* She played it straight, and she played it well. And now she'll be unemployed, and she'll have to go join the ranks of the aspiring. She was good, indeed.

Martusciello arrived at the police station. Standing at the entrance to the building was the same police officer as earlier:

"Did you find what you left in the subway?"

"No, but I did find pieces of other things that I'd lost. It's one of those things that happens."

Outside the door to his office, the captain saw two women seated, waiting for him. He guessed their ages as, one, thirty or so, the other, almost fifty but a very nice fifty. The thirty-year-old kept moving her legs: crossing them, stretching them out in front of her, tapping the pavement, exercising her calves by flexing her feet. The almost-fifty-year-old was arranging the contents of her purse, as if to make up for the time she was wasting while waiting for him. She gave him a smile.

Martusciello reached for the door handle.

"You can't go in. Apparently we have to wait our turn."

"I work here, they won't be mad at me."

And he went through the door.

Blanca, Liguori, and a woman with short hair were sitting on the same side of his desk, talking. His office chair was empty, and a cigarette lighter seemed to be holding his place.

Liguori walked toward him and asked him where he'd been. The captain smiled, distantly, challenging the detective's habit of being the first to make a move.

"I drank a cup of coffee with a serial killer who waters plants."

Blanca turned formal.

"At Captain Malanò's request, we've summoned Signora Rosina Mastriani, present in this room, Signora Mara Scacchi, and Signora Julia Marin. All three women have had contact with the victim."

"Well, go ahead in that case. Never let me be one to thwart Malanò's purposes."

Signora Rosina Mastriani caught Martusciello's annoyance. She caught it because she felt the same way.

"Captain, Vialdi had countless women. But I wasn't seeing him anymore, because I'm never comfortable standing in line so I generally just give up and go away."

Blanca nodded. Liguori noticed the sergeant's gesture and moved closer to Rosina Mastriani.

"We'll summon the countless women to come in too. Signora Mastriani, present in this room," he went on, imitating Blanca's phrase and then glancing over at Martusciello, "was just telling us about Vialdi."

"Well, Signora, if it's not too much trouble, could you repeat for me what you told my colleagues?"

"Vialdi was a creep."

"May his soul rest in peace," Liguori commented.

"He's dead, more power to him, but when he was still alive he played a considerable role in ruining my life. He was a friend of my husband's, he came to see me. I fell for him."

Liguori was about to add a further comment, but the captain beat him to it.

"Go on, Signora."

"I'm forty-two years old, but I wasn't born yesterday: I left my husband and children and went to live on my own."

"At Vialdi's place?"

"I wasn't invited. He said that nothing kills love like a routine."

This time Martusciello wasn't quick enough to keep Liguori from talking; the detective whispered for Blanca's benefit:

"Anna Karenina is tearing up the pages. One by one."

"Did you say something, Detective?"

"Nothing, Signora."

Rosina Mastriani shrugged her shoulders.

"That's how it went. I held out for three years, I stayed in the apartment I had rented, and I went on with my life."

The captain, apprehensive of the glance that he expected from Liguori, asked her:

"Was there anyone who could have benefited from his death? Did he have any ties with organized crime?" The detective turned his hands palm upward and fanned his fingers to show his discomfort. The standard questions struck him as so much boilerplate.

"How would I know?"

Rosina Mastriani stopped to think.

"I do know that everything and everyone was a plaything to him: gambling, bills, horses, soccer." She broke off again. "For a while, he loved cars, then he stopped caring about them. He had countless women."

"So you said," Liguori observed.

"Sorry about that, I tend to repeat myself. Can I go now?" Liguori walked her to the door and handed her a card with his office numbers.

13.

A nna Karenina. You use the books you read like some obnoxious handgun," Martusciello said to Liguori once the three of them were alone. "You're one of those intolerant snobs dripping rancid venom on all the citizens who are incapable of repeating the things you say, or learning the things you know."

"That's so untrue. I'm fond of you actually."

"Drop dead, but do it slowly. And by the way, excuse me but aren't your offices suitable for interviewing people?"

"No, put the blame for that on me," Blanca stepped in. "On our side of the building, they're reinforcing the eaves of the building and I was afraid I wouldn't be able to hear clearly because of the construction noise."

"Blanca, give me a break: you can hear the anchovies in the harbor breathing. And in any case, what did you hear?"

"Nothing significant. I noticed some hesitancy when she mentioned gambling. She modified her tone of voice, she laid a little more emphasis on her vowels, she stalled for time. Either she lied, or there's something connected to it that makes her uncomfortable. That aside, the few phrases she spoke strike me as consistent. What's she like?"

"What do you mean what's she like?" Liguori asked.

"What's she like physically?"

"Oh, right. I always forget that you . . . Let me think it over."

"Well, think it over and tell me what she's like."

"I don't know, if she kept her mouth shut she might be all

right. Red hair, cropped short, but the hair color's pretty close to the original: she has some freckles along her neckline that confirm the color. She kept touching her nose, slender waist, long legs. Her fingernails are chipped along the edges, she has a scent of France gone sour."

"My nose works fine."

Martusciello sensed a tension between the two of them, like a couple of promised lovers who had limited themselves only to promises for too long.

"What do you say we bring the other two women in together? It's already three o'clock."

Liguori walked over to open the door.

Mara Scacchi strode in, clearly eager to get done and leave as quickly as possible. She went on moving her legs even once she was seated on the chair that Liguori had been using.

Julia Marin took a seat and rummaged through her purse for her sunglasses. She justified herself:

"I can't stand the light."

Blanca turned her head in the direction of the older woman, who was unaware of her limited vision:

"From the Veneto?"

"Yes, I'm from Verona. I come . . . I come to Naples frequently for . . . But now I live in Verona and that's where I'm going to stay. As soon as I get out of this police station I'm returning home."

Liguori studied her profile: her mouth, her hair, her straight back, her stockings, black, a little out of season.

Martusciello noticed Liguori's interest and gave him free rein. He was good with women—for Martusciello's taste, a little too good.

"We're sorry to have forced you to come back to such painful surroundings, but we know that you were very important to Jerry Vialdi."

"I hope so. In any case, Gennaro—that's what I preferred

to call him, I never liked his stage name—was certainly important to me. I know that I might seem like a fool, but I'm endowed with an elaborate form of emotional idiocy. It's unbelievable how many years the man made me waste."

"Me too." Mara Scacchi's voice sounded shrill. "Useless years of wating and time wasted. He would summon his lovers to his concerts, and he'd dedicate songs and long lingering looks to each woman. He may even have doled out his attention in alphabetical order. He'd stand me up for one date after another. I always seemed to be somewhere waiting for him, he was worse than the Mergellina-Posillipo bus."

Julia Marin lowered her dark glasses to get a better look at the woman who'd interrupted her. Liguori appreciated the knowing seductiveness of her hands and eyes.

"That's not what I meant. Gennaro took years away from me, true enough, but mainly in the sense that he made me forget how old I was. I knew that he saw other women. I'm not saying that I didn't care, but it only mattered to a certain extent. I was happy with a very imperfect situation, and I held tight to it. I even went along with his fear of oneness, of loving just one woman. I said it before: I verge on a form of idiot wisdom. I miss Gennaro. I understand that you might be particularly interested in this taste of geriatric honey. What else do you want to know?"

The melodious Venetian accent had taken Blanca to a lovely place, a place of great calm. With carefully chosen words the sergeant asked both women about Vialdi's business dealings, about how he was able to wear different hats, professionally speaking.

With differing tones of voice and intentions, the women confirmed Rosina Mastriani's information. The final conclusion fell to Mara Scacchi.

"Enemies? Sure he had them, but they weren't all that ferocious."

"Are you by any chance a psychologist?" asked Liguori.

"No, I'm a pharmacist. All I meant was that Jerry wasn't even all that good at getting people to hate him."

Martusciello didn't appreciate the comment.

"Signora, believe me, he was very good at getting someone to hate him."

14

Blanca stood up to see Mara Scacchi and Julia Marin to the door. She brushed her hands along the edge of everything she encountered.

Liguori watched her as she left the room; he rested his eyes on the pale white nape of the neck, the shoulders, the waist, the feral hips of a woman who can run even in pitch darkness.

Martusciello noticed his gaze:

"Let her be, Liguori."

"Jealous?"

Mara Scacchi hurried off.

Julia Marin extended her hand to say farewell to the sergeant. Blanca overlooked the movement of the woman's arm: she was still distracted by the detective's gaze on her back.

Julia Marin stood there, motionless and uncertain, and only then did it dawn on her that the policewoman must have some problem with her sight.

"Well, I'm leaving, I'm heading back to Verona, if . . . "

Blanca sensed the variation in the woman's voice and connected it to the sense of embarrassment previously experienced by others who had noticed her eyes. She knew the diverse array of rections by heart: some displayed something verging on annoyance that they hadn't been previously informed, as if it were her duty to wear a highway sign announcing limited visibility hanging around her neck. Others, the majority, started talking to her in simpler words, enunciating more clearly. To them, partial blindness turned her into a child who was also hard of hearing. And others diluted their words into diminutives, in a display of saccharine courtesy. Nearly all of them avoided stating exactly what they'd understood, beating around the bush to a ridiculous extent. Nearly all of them. But none of them knew just how unpredictable her darkness could be. A switch, over which she had no control, could suddenly flip and give her a much more accurate outline of the shadows. It was a mystery, this ungovernable ability. She often told herself that the lack or the intensification of light might be a result of weariness, her mood, everyday irritations, but then there were times when the images came to see her just when she was as at her weakest and most out of sorts.

And so she'd resigned herself to the cruel whim of chance, said nothing, and obeyed changes she was helpless to guide or direct.

Julia Marin called her back to the present and surprised her.

"I'm so sorry, I didn't realize."

"It almost never happens that someone says to me *I didn't realize*." She laughed. "I feel like a cup of tea. Would you care to join me? Would you like something? Right next door there's a famous four-star tea room."

"Gladly."

Blanca strode confidently toward the little broom closet that Càrita had set up as the office bar and coffee shop.

Ever since Giuseppe Càrita had chosen to tread the path of Art, a sense of desuetude had hovered over the broom closet. The checkered oilcloth no longer gleamed and the tins and bottles were in disarray. Still, it offered the considerable advantage of free access, which in past moments of greater glamor and coffee Càrita would never have permitted.

As she watched Blanca move confidently to put the kettle

on the fire and prepare the teacups, Julia Marin quickly and easily forgot.

Blanca, in the restricted space, was better able to recognize the woman's calm presence.

"You strike as somehow distant. Just the right degree, frankly. Despite your recent loss."

"That's right. What is left is my prerogative to say and do what at the moment strikes me as the lesser evil. In any case it won't change a thing. What I did for a living was organize concerts, in my private life I was always a negotiator, I've always been mild mannered and quick to give up. Then I met Gennaro. He desired me with an arrogance that I loved. Perhaps it was a question of age. Perhaps, for the first time, I made a decision. I couldn't say. But I went ahead and bothered to choose the death that in any case will certainly come along sooner or later in this kind of a love affair. Only in this case, what came along was a death of the flesh." She dropped her voice. "My body's dead too, the years all came rushing back together, with compound interest. Excuse me." Blanca shredded three mint leaves into her tea and then sniffed her fingers. The pleasure spread to her mouth. Death could still make her furious with life and with despite.

"Who did it, Julia?"

"I can guess, but I won't say. It's too late. Don't try to push me, we're alone, I'll deny everything. Or else I'll surprise you, who can say? Why don't you come see me? I'll let you hear the sound of the river Adige running under the bridges. Beautiful." Julia Marin took Blanca's hand to say farewell. "See you again soon. You are a very pretty woman." Blanca sought with her fingertips the wrinkles on the back of the other woman's hand.

"I don't believe that and in any case I'd have no way of knowing, my memory of me dates back to when I was thirteen. I don't know what I've turned into. In any case, beauty would just be one more luxury that I can hardly afford. It was a pleasure to meet you."

Julia Marin went back to her hotel to get her luggage. She didn't have much time before she was due at the central station.

They'd given her the usual room.

She went to the window that overlooked both the entrance and the Bay of Naples. With distant eyes she stared at the water as if it weren't the sea, then she looked at the trellis of bougainvillea and jasmine that ran along the entry drive.

She remembered every step she'd taken along that drive with Vialdi at her side, the laughter, the girlish excitement as she gave her ID to the desk clerk, the sound of her heels on the stairs, the hasty kisses before entering the hotel room. She closed her eyes and saw all the rest that could no longer touch her.

She left her clothes in the closet.

She arranged two toothbrushes in the bathroom.

"I brought you one, you always forget yours." She sat down on the bed and looked through her purse with its well organized contents for her telephone.

"This is Julia Marin. I'm well aware that you know about me. I have something to say to you."

15.

When they stuck the knife into your neck, I was there. It was a beautiful day, the Phlegraean light had been rinsed in the clear salt water, and not even a shadow could survive in the bright air.

It's something I've noticed, the worst things that have happened to me have often had beautiful landscapes as backdrops. Perhaps the joyous panorama is doing its best to highlight the lovely spread legs of bloody wounds. Which isn't such a bad thing. You know, I've always loved contrasts.

There. Now they're going to kill him, now they're going to kill him.

They're going to kill my father, my brother, my beloved one. Now they're going to rid the earth of what remains of my face, my only smile; I'll shuffle off this coil lost in a delirium of hours seized by the tapeworms that consume wakefulness and slumber.

The man who had his arms around your shoulders sunk in the knife and gave it half a pirouette twirl.

A slow drop oozed down your neck.

The other man laughed:

"Look out, you're going to get his nice shirt all bloody."

"What does that matter? He can always buy himself another. With our money he can buy it."

You weren't talking, you had red fear in the corners of your eyes.

"Three days," they told you before leaving.

The knife had left the faintest embroidery on you, they knew how to do their work: you might have just nicked yourself shaving.

I know every detail of your neck and I was relieved, you weren't dead and your skin would repair the embroidery.

You went off onto the terrace. I followed you. You were ashamed of your tears and the rancid stench of your own terror.

"Get away from me. Wait for me in the house."

I waited.

You came back after an hour, lowered the blinds, shut the curtains, and turned off all the lights.

The voice arrived from a precise place I couldn't see:

"Now you get over there and do what you're supposed to do, my little man."

"At your orders, sir."

16.

Martusciello put the chairs back in place. His own untidiness was more than enough.

Years of thinking about investigations had carved a rut: the captain left his office, as was his custom, pondering the people he had just met:

Three women in three years, plus the thousands on the side. What a robust constitution that Vialdi had. Bursting with health and cocaine, I'd be tempted to say. The older woman, Marin, has the tick tock of death in her eyes. Still, a nice kind of death, and I have to say that I like women who have the passing years stamped into their bodies. The other two each have thighs that make you hide in the first empty hole you see. Better yet if it's solid gold. Hasty approximations tend to toss a series of *this*, *that*, and *the other thing* in your face. They have the *why* and the *how* stamped on their chests. In any case, I don't give a damn about any of it, not even about this envy of mine. I don't want to know, I don't want to add two plus two, I don't even want my head venturing into the logic of the facts; anyway, logic is finite, and facts are misleading. I'm only amazed that no excruciating interviewer has come to torment me in the midst of this vast expanse of nothingness.

Giuseppe Càrita knocked and cleared his throat.

"Captain, forgive my intrusion, but there's a woman, the journalist Chetruli from *Free World Weekly*, who wants to have a word."

"Precisely where my mind was at. So let her have her word, remove the duct tape from her face."

"No, Captain, she wants to talk directly to you."

"Unfortunately, Peppino, her desire is not mutual."

"Giuseppe."

"Peppino, do something for me: send her to Liguori."

"At your orders, Captain."

"Ah, Peppino, one more thing. I'm ill suited to this theater of yours. I don't like it. Unless you cut it out, playing the policeman who's playing a policeman, what I'm going to do is toss you out on your ear, ship you off to some other police station, maybe on the far side of nowhere."

"Captain, sir, you have no heart, with all due respect, sir, really you don't understand."

"No, I don't understand a thing. And the older I get, the less I understand. It's not true that your horizons broaden as you get older! The dripping drops of days have carved a hole," and Martusciello pointed to the top of his forehead. "There's a leak right here and the rain gets in, along with everything else, and it all turns into a churning muck."

"You see, you don't understand. Why, did you know that even Funicella Corta has found another role?"

"You don't say! Just how big is the theater? Does it seat many?"

"No, it's in an auto repair shop. Do you remember Funicella Corta?"

"He's not that idiot who got tangled up in explosives at the store of the fellow who was late on his kickbacks?"

"That's right, Captain, he's the one. He lost three fingers. You turned him into an informant. Do you remember?"

"Carità, skip the *do you remember* routine, you're starting to sound like some ad for omega-3."

"Well, what of it? He's taking the course too. And you ought to see the good it's done him: he's a new man."

"Ah, the resurrection of Funicella Corta."

"You know who sent him to my maestro? None other than your murder victim."

"Who, Vialdi? Peppi', Vialdi's by no means *my* murder victim, in fact he belongs to Captain Malanò, or perhaps to Detective Liguori."

"Captain, whoever he may belong to is who he belongs to. I know for certain that Funicella is very grateful to him."

"So how's he making a living these days? I have to guess he's not living on ticket receipts."

"No, he's not working with the girls anymore. He does a little small-time dope peddling for the Sconciglio family."

"Peppino, do you have rehearsals at your theater tonight?"

"We start in an hour."

"And will Funicella be there?"

"He generally comes. A little late, but he comes."

"Then we'll see you later at the auto repair shop. Now go tell this Chetruli from *Free Fucking World Weekly* that True Art is a-callin'. Tell her to go see Liguori."

Martusciello quickly threw on his jacket and left the officer, practically running headlong into Chetruli.

"Captain, I was waiting for you. Is it true that for the Vialdi murder you've already questioned three likely serial murderesses? We've heard rumors that among the suspects there is a good-looking and slightly perverse woman from out of town." Chetruli pronounced "perverse" with gusto. "Tell me everything. I want to know."

"Detective Liguori will be delighted to help your scratch your humanitarian itches. Deputy Giuseppe Càrita is here merely to show you the way. He lives for such occasions."

17

A t the front door of the police station, a chilly north wind reinforced Martusciello's decision to walk to the auto repair shop/theater.

The sudden chill helped him to put a certain enjoyable distance between himself and the unpleasant summer, the creaking swing of boredom that would accompany him all the way home.

Santina was spending more and more time at her conferences at the History Institute, and she usually came home late. He'd eat dinner, alone, watching a game. What I'd like to know is why she wants to spend all her time with those egghead women, he thought. Forty-year-old babies who live in dorms, four or five to a room, their groceries all split up and marked in the refrigerator, their shares of the rent stretched out, and the barley shake watered down to nothing by the end of the month, the bathroom adorned with different brands of toilet paper. To each her own: separate needs. It's not their fault, sure, I understand that, it's the fault of these betrayals of homeland and country, but I'm sick of all this innocence already going into retirement. And perhaps they really have infected Santina with their years of stale adolescence. Now she's fixated with Benedetto Croce, and she studies. She has this fascination with legends. Santina studies and studies and never thinks of the cross. And I'm sure she's doing the right thing, let everyone deal with their own disasters. I never thought I'd wind up like this. I never imagined it. I held tight

to some sense of pity and a tufa-stone heart. Spongy. I must
have forgotten it somewhere, or else it wore itself out after all
the times it's been slammed face-first into the wall. *You complain about having too much*, you'd probably say. And you'd be
right, Santina. You got rid of the ugliness of life, hid it from
your eyes, while I practically made love to it. One minor satisfaction would be the opportunity to wreck Malanò's plans,
ruin the fun he's hoping to have with this carousel of serial
murders. Make him slip and fall on his ass, trip over a bitter
piece of hard motive, ideally money, because in the end money
tends to hang its murders on the hook next to the usual set of
scales for weighing gold. Every so often, yes, someone kills out
of love, an argument with a neighbor, or even by mistake. But
money still takes the top podium and the Olympic gold. Even
your little schoolmarm friends would cut each others' throats
for a house by the sea like Vialdi's. Whatever. Instead of the
unspeakable appendage that they took from me at the
Ultramarine clinic, they should have removed certain scars.
I've seen too many things, I have. Even still, I keep reaching
out for Santina, but I don't know what's become of her either.
It's okay, I'll be able to deal with it. Let's go see if we can't
wreck Malanò's plans.

The captain's feet were freezing in his thin socks. The bru-
tal north wind turned them into chunks of ice.

The shops were filling up, the chill had caught light shirts
and sandals unawares. Pedestrians were seeking shelter.

The captain wandered away from the noise of the little
shops to climb the hill to the women's prison. The building
was a fifteenth-century convent that had been turned into a
penitentiary. There it stood, still intact, beautiful and immor-
tal, in spite of the frequent seismic shocks and the bones contained within.

Martusciello stopped outside the entrance, lit a cigarette
and murmured to himself *always save women and children first.*

He smiled nastily and reflected that the two prisons, one on Nisida and the other in Pozzuoli, managed to remain still in the midst of all this beauty, even though it seemed as if they were about to vanish from one moment to the next.

The sea responded by hurling huge, dangerous waves onto the quay, chasing away everyone on foot.

The auto repair shop/theater reeked of dampness, grease, gasoline, and insecticide. A blend that clutched Martusciello's empty stomach and squeezed it into a clenched fist of vomit. He looked around, but nobody asked him anything; often relatives acted as spectators for other relatives on the hard road to art.

The school was located in a space that must once have been a storage area. You walked down into the room by a rickety worm-eaten wooden staircase. On the walls were a series of mismatched mirrors, taken from a succession of dressers and credenzas from different eras, all reflecting the groups of aspiring actors. Because of the dank air, the women were wearing old-fashioned leg warmers and headbands and shawls and light skirts over heavy woolen stockings, in a crèche-like arrangement that had been assembled at home and was out of season. The men wore jackets and ties fished out of storage: sleeves too wide, trousers too tight. All of it churning in a hubbub of excitement that struck Martusciello as even more out of place and out of season than the manger scene.

The theatrical maestro showed up, decked out in Borsalino hat and oversized radio. He clapped his hands a couple of times.

"All right, kids!" When he heard the word "kids," the captain's stomach was released, the fist unclenched. If anything, he wished he could land that fist square on the maestro's skinny face. "Those other actors, the ones at the other garage/ theater school, are getting a bigger enrollment than we are. We have to shake off the humiliation. This performance will have to be perfect. I want the theater to collapse from the applause. Tonight, we're going to do an extra fifteen minutes, it's my gift to you."

"What luck," Martusciello murmured under his breath.

18.

To keep from giving in to his anger and melancholy, the captain walked out into the alley.

He saw Giuseppe Càrita arrive, afflicted with a skintight tracksuit.

"Ah, so you're not wearing a tuxedo."

"No, I'm one of the leads. I have to be dressed differently. It has to be obvious."

"So you decided to dress as a worm."

Giuseppe Càrita puffed out his chest in pride:

"I'm Time dancing on History."

"Ah, I see. I'd missed that detail."

"You said it yourself, sir, lately you don't understand a blessed thing. Right down to the soles of your feet, you have a bitterness about you that smacks of gall and wormwood. Begging your pardon for the observation."

"Be careful when you tread those boards. They're looking mighty creaky."

Martusciello smiled and lit himself a cigarette. Ever since he'd rescinded the order to smoke no more than three of them he enjoyed the pleasure of tobacco from the moment he stuck his hand into his pocket in search of his lighter. And he repeated the act every time he felt the urge, offending his spongy heart with the appetite that he was about to gratify.

Funicella Corta came in half an hour later. He pretended he hadn't seen the captain and tried to rush into the auto repair shop. Martusciello stepped in front of him.

"What's this, Funicella, have you already forgotten you know me?"

"Captain, with due respect, you are not easily forgettable."

"Let's go get a cup of coffee. I miss the stories you tell. Love will do that to you."

"I have theater class."

"Have it the way you prefer. Then we'll talk tomorrow at the police station. If you'd rather, I can send an officer with a squad car to pick you up."

"I suddenly feel this urge for coffee."

The two men headed off toward a bar. Along the way, neither man spoke, Funicella keeping a safe distance from the captain.

"What are you going to have, Funicella?"

"What are you thinking?—it's my treat. Captain, what do you want to know?"

"Let's see if you can guess."

"I'm going to ask you to do me this favor, let's not start up tonight with these half-baked daisy chains of questions designed to wear me out, I'm not sure I'm up for it this evening."

"And you have a point, but that's just the way village donkeys do. They have the patience of centuries as beasts of burden, nothing to be done about it. But did you seriously ask me what I want to know, Funicella?"

"I give up. You want to know about Vialdi."

"You may not be much at handling explosives, but to make up for it you know how to read minds. That's something, anyway."

"I hear that he was murdered by a killer from out of town. One of the ones that get off on seeing dead bodies, and so when they don't have one handy they start thinking about it all on their own. On the Internet there's lots about this kind of stuff."

"Actor, *killer*, Internet. Aren't you becoming sophisticated!"

"Captain, I have to try to keep up with the times, I only have one life to live."

"Not me, I'm reincarnated on a regular basis, the only thing that remains each time is the feet, which is why they're so worn out. Funice', who do you think this killer from out of town could be?"

"How would I know! It could even be one of the women who've passed through your hands."

"Ah, I see that you're well informed, as always. But do you remember when we came to pick you up, half dead, outside of the shop?" The man waved his fingerless hand in front of the captain's face. "I set two officers to guard you at the hospital: whoever sent you to burn down that shop was probably interested in making sure you lost your tongue as well as your fingers. I arranged to circulate a rumor that you hadn't talked and that you weren't about to. So you were able to do your prison time without poison. I caught your bosses, the ones who were responsible for the arson, but you came out of it clean as a whistle."

"You were like a father to me."

"Funice', I have a daughter and a niece, and they're enough, way more than enough. I'm going to repeat the question: what can you tell me about Vialdi?"

"What do you want to know?"

"Everything."

"Everything I know?"

"Sure, but add anything you can imagine to the mix. Let yourself go. You know, I never believed that you screwed up that bomb yourself. I always suspected that they gave you a little help in getting your calculations wrong, on account of that scheming heart of yours. You were already evolving, even before the theater and the Internet. In fact, now you're working for the Sconciglio family, just think of that, you have a new boss."

"What are you trying to tell me? I don't get it."

"Then let me make it a little clearer to you. You snuck into the household of another boss so you could pilfer information about the cash flows in and around the port of Naples. Everyone has their own bridge over the Strait, their own infinite horizon. You were willing to stoop so low as to become a hired arson-hand, just so you could pass yourself off as a willing gopher for the Sconciglios. Funicella, I don't think you're a two-bit discard. I think you know things. So I think you want to tell me what you know."

"It's not your case. It belongs to Malanò from Fuorigrotta."

"You see what an amazing amount of things you know?"

"Captain, I deal a little pot for Sconciglio. You're getting it all wrong."

"Maybe so. So why don't you get everything wrong too, and start talking?"

"Captain, I'm working on imagination here, but if you ask me, success went in Jerry Vialdi's mouth and dissolved all his natural prudence: women, men, cars, lots of money, a little bit of excellent dope, excursions out of the country, horses, whopping bills, an insult here, an insult there. Maybe he started to think he was a little too independent and he forgot where he came up from. He started out singing at first communions, you know that. He'd specialized. At the time, he earned two million lire a night. Tax free. He was born in the Sanità neighborhood, his mother was Concetta Mangiavento known as Sette Carceri—Seven Prisons—because every one of her seven sons was in a different prison. The fathers had no fixed address or even any established identity. Once Vialdi achieved success, he took mother and brothers and flew them off to South America, more to get them out of his hair than out of any great love of family. He wanted to wash his face and spruce up his image so he started working with that ugly thing, Gatta Mignon, poor woman. She's the one who helped him make the great leap forward, and she tended to him like a priest tends to his altar. She even taught him how to dress, she put the right words in his mouth. In other words, she gave birth to him all over again, better than even Sette Carceri could have done. And that's that."

"Your fantasy is incomplete. Why was he killed? What you're telling is all stuff I already knew, it's not enough."

"I can't help you there. Let's go back to square one, maybe it was a bloodthirsty *killer*," he said, leaning on the exotic English word.

"The same mistake as always. Everyone makes the same mistake with me. They see me as the village donkey and say to themselves *now I'm going to see if he'll swallow some unlikely story, after all he's nothing but a stupid donkey!* Not the horse, the horse can't be that stupid, but the donkey, sure: he's always there, at the edge of the cliff, takes a beating but won't step aside, doesn't kick when they pile a load on his back that's no good to him, so there's no question: the donkey must be stupid. Funicella, in this land of ours, the bloodthirsty killers, the ones who do their killing strictly to satisfy a gluttonous whim, are in clear danger of being towed out to sea and abandoned to the currents that run south to Africa. A certain independence in terms of managing the easy disposing of troublesome headaches is afforded to Chinese businessmen, but in order to gain that independence they'd had to pay import tariffs on their counterfeit designer labels. The Nigerians, provided they don't overstep their bounds and they keep to their assigned territory, are permitted to do as much street vending of this and that as they want, if they pay of course a hefty indemnity, while the Albanians pop into and out of the negotiations, but strictly with a few historic families with a stinking reputation and escutcheon. No two ways about it: all of them are obliged to pass under the gallows of the native bosses around here. Sure, there might be an occasional exception, but even though I am a donkey, it still strikes me as very odd that a recording artist, the son of none other than Sette Carceri, as it happens, should just happen to run headlong into the one unsettling exception. I don't believe in it. Who do you think he is, John Lennon?"

"But listen, Captain, if a restless killer gathers his courage and wants to eliminate someone who neither helps nor hinders, why should certain surnames take it the wrong way?"

Martusciello froze. The time he spent with Blanca had taught him a thing or two about tones of voice. The voice of his confidential informant was unmistakably veined with traces of sincerity.

"Is this fantasy or history?"

"No, Captain, I told you before, this is all pure fantasy. I still have one hand, the only thing the other one is good for is to brush away the flies of stray thoughts in my brain."

"Sure, I follow you, you only have one life and one hand." He pulled a crumpled business card out of his pocket. "And also one telephone number, my personal line. Let me know about any fresh fantasies, the minute they arrive. Ah, and if by any chance you happen to run into the head of the Sconciglio family, please tell him that this serial killer nonsense is trying my nerves. Let's have him abort all the nonsense circulating inside Malanò's head."

"Let's see if that's all the nonsense there is there."

On the way back, Martusciello told himself that feet and head had both obeyed the imposition of new ideas. So, obliging them to do a little exercise had been beneficial.

He got off at Piazza Garibaldi, and took the long way home, which allowed him to walk past the Albergo dei Poveri, Naples's old poorhouse.

In the eighteenth century, paupers didn't have the luxury of sleeping in the underpasses of the subway system; rather, there was a building equipped to house some eight thousand homeless people.

The monumental white façade made the palm trees below look like slender blades of grass, and the present-day even thinner than the palm trees.

He limped off, poetic justice inflicting a sharp pain to his heel.

Santina welcomed him home with a relaxed smile, Benedetto Croce must have done her good:

"Where have you been till this time of night?"

"At the theater."

19.

"What did you do?"

Sergio looked at Blanca, sitting next to him in the car.

"I don't want to talk about it."

He thumbed through the MP3 player hooked up to the car radio and stopped on *Killers*, by Iron Maiden.

"Put in your earbuds, Sergio. I can't take it."

"Oooh, aren't you in a sociable mood. Nini told me to tell you that you're going to have a guest: one of her girlfriends, Tita, will be staying with you. Nini, Tita: never a girl with a name like Assunta or Patrizia."

"Tita is the diminutive of Assunta."

The kid stuck a single earbud in his ear. After a short while the other earbud, dangling on his chest, droned: *A voice inside me compelling to satisfy me.* Blanca traced the sound, grabbed the earbud, and stuck it into his other ear:

"I told you I can't take it."

In his search for a parking place, Sergio drove a couple of times around the stadium. He turned off the MP3 player.

"Sometimes I've just got to hear a song, that one song and no other. Then I turn it off, wait ten minutes, and play it again. Full volume, no earbuds. I could go on like that for hours. I fixate on a couple of lines and wait for them. Like: *Scream for mercy, he laughs as he's watching you bleed...* How do you think I'd do as a cop?"

"What does that have to do with anything, right now?"

"Nothing. It's just that sometimes I worry about the years going by and me sitting here, same as ever, going nowhere, in other words. I'm looking around for an emergency exit."

"'Nice victory, then, is yours! In cases like this, you should give flowers to policemen, my friends.' You know who said that?"

"Search me."

"You should give flowers to policemen, not leftovers. My addition. Why don't you go find out who said it, I'm not going to tell you. Here where we live, the only possible revolution would involve following the rules, but it bothers me even to think about explaining it to you."

"Whatever you say, Auntie. But you want to know something? When you come back from work, it's like you left a piece of yourself there. You're a mess."

"You obviously sleep too late. Even at this hour of the night, you're still talking and talking. See you tomorrow. And try to be punctual."

Blanca took her shoes off on the landing and went in without making noise. She managed to move with slow, controlled silent motions.

She felt a need for solitude. She put her purse on the couch and went into the kitchen, sticking her hands under a trickle of soundless water, and then ran them over her arms. She did the same thing for the benefit of her forehead, her mouth, and the back of her neck. Her hands were her mirror, her way of recognizing her vital boundaries in the absence of a gaze.

Night and home took her back into a closed shell where she could rest. Where she could surrender.

She got some leftovers and a glass of red wine and sat on the floor, near the half-empty door that gave onto the terrace.

The muggy air turned her a little feral. She ate without silverware, quick bites, licking the crystal glass and the solitude she'd sought. *Blanca, when you come back from work, it's like you left a piece of yourself there*. She told herself that she needed to stop letting Liguori invade her personal space. It was starting to become obvious.

She glimpsed a flash that lit up the stadium through the glass: once again, uncertainty whether it was deception or actual perception. The truce had been short-lived.

She couldn't seem to tell whether the image did or didn't correspond to the landscape. She thought she could see a diffuse light illuminating the oval of the upper perimeter, the exterior structures, and the slight upward tilt of the pavement. Then the flash became the usual blaze and died out without warning. Blanca tried to bring back the image, but all she was able to master, with an exhausting effort of her eyes, was a high halo that could even have come from the moon.

She blamed it all on Liguori.

Impulses that should remain in the depths multiply in you, and because of you. Dark impulses. I don't want to concede anything to you, least of all the laborious answer to my troubles. I don't want anything from you. Do you hear me? *I don't want anything from you*. The intention did no good, in fact, if anything, it made the thoughts race faster. So she found herself yearning to kiss him long and slow, to learn the other tongue with her own, the faint wrinkles of his lips.

Blanca needed to find a distraction. And so she focused on her work: an inspection of the stadium, that's what she needed now. The next morning she'd ask Sergio to take her there. But first she'd have to ask Malanò's permission. She already knew that Martusciello wasn't going to like it.

The pounding and the flavors faded to a tolerable intensity.

She got a blanket and stretched out on the couch; she'd sleep there. She had no desire to lose what little sleepiness remained to her.

She heard Nini's voice. She'd forgotten to say hello.

She got up and headed back to the girl's bedroom, barefoot. As she turned into the hallway a whispered phrase wafted toward her:

"You need to calm down, Tita. What do you think they're going to do now: kill all of Vialdi's women? That's impossible."

Blanca froze, slowed her respiration, and waited to hear more.

"What if the serial killer really exists? How would we know? All I know is that my mother's turned into a ghost: skinny, ravenous, and stupid. Did you know that she even told my father? Now, I know that he's not much, but to hear that your wife is head-over-heels in love with some bastard singer, neomelodic, and dead to boot, is too much even for him! I can't take it anymore. I wish I'd picked better parents. Still, I'm sorry for her and I don't want her to die."

"Keep your voice down, if Blanca comes home she'll hear everything."

"But we're whispering! Plus the music's playing. You're just paranoid."

"My mother can even hear me dreaming."

"Your mother? But isn't your mother someone else?"

"Sure, Margherita, but my real mother was also a daughter. Blanca is a mother and nothing else. It's hard to explain. I have two mothers and zero fathers, that's just how it went. You want me to tell her about it? She's a policewoman, you know."

Blanca felt the word *mother* throbbing in her temples. It pounded all the way into the bonfires of her eyes: *mother, mother, mother*. She'd never heard the girl utter that word.

"Don't even think about it, Nini."

Blanca went and put on her shoes and then entered Nini's room, making sure the sound of her footsteps announced her well ahead of time.

"Hi, what are you two up to?"

"Nothing, just talking. I didn't hear you come in. I didn't hear the sound of the door closing."

She leaned over Nini, kissed her cheek, and breathed in her wisteria scent.

Nini walked out of the room with some excuse so she could leave her alone with Tita: she was hoping her friend would take advantage of this opportunity to confide her fear. She went into the kitchen, saw the plate in the sink, the terrace door left ajar. On her way back, she noticed the blanket on the couch.

"She heard everything," she thought.

20

From his office window, Detective Liguori was watching Blanca as she stood motionless outside the police station's front door.

Sergio got out of the car and walked toward her. She spurned his help, brushed the car door with her body, identified the appropriate movement, which struck Liguori as particularly graceful, and got into the car.

The young man's helpless stance as he waited, his rapid strides around the car to the driver's side, the hand extending out the window to adjust the rearview mirror, all reminded the detective of his own youthful hesitations.

Not that they're by any means all gone now, he thought, but the emptiness where they once existed has since been filled in. There've been countless moves, sheddings of skin, annoying starts, the choice of a scandalous line of work that, when you come right down to it, I don't quite get what all the scandal is about, the satisfaction of knowing how many people I was able to dissatisfy, including myself. The latest companion did her best to sweep away the prior couplings. Not very successfully, but she did do her best. She left, perhaps for someplace safe. Soon relief took the place of pining and yearning and the various vicinities all filled in. I've stopped trying to clear up misunderstandings and I've begun, once again, to cultivate them. So much the better, because I'm no good at pretending to encourage ramshackle ambitions of eternity. A slice here, another nugget there, a quick dismissal after many long hours of enjoyment, rapid mental seductions, subsequently discarded. For now, I just go on arguing in favor of marvelous chaos, and with time we'll see what happens. If Martusciello could hear this line of thought, he'd probably shoot me. Tonight, I just don't feel like going home.

He switched on his cell phone and selected the right message according to his present whims.

He found himself in Via Duomo with Carolina, a long-standing friend of well-established amorous detachment; he had accepted the invitation for an evening's entertainment in a small theater, fifty seats, in one of the numerous Neapolitan middle grounds between city center and far-flung hinterland.

Liguori decided that in any case he'd enjoy himself, that he'd even tolerate the chic evangelistic pedantry of the cultured nothingness. The frenzy for life that he'd rediscovered in himself gave him a sense of speed and pleasure. For him, that was enough to make it a fun night out.

They started off into the warren of alleys and lanes, allowing themselves to be surprised by the piazzas, unexpected occasions for spaces, and the successive narrowings where historic palazzi, solemn and tumbledown, once again brushed cornice against cornice.

"Did you know that lately I don't even feel like such a foreigner? What a wonderful thing."

"Next you'll be sloughing off boredom and indifference, at which point I won't even recognize you anymore. Or else they'll eat you alive."

"So what's this evening's show about?"

"It's a monologue based on the Saramago novel *Blindness*. The actess is really good, Santina D'Offerta. She's a friend, I'll introduce you after the show."

"Let's hope for the best," the detective laughed. "Your friend happens to have the same name as my boss's wife."

"And what's so odd about that?"

"Well, Santina is hardly a common name."

In the small space in front of the ticket office they stood alone. Liguori and Carolina looked around them with the embarrassment of a mistaken appointment.

The detective had not lost the desire to be there. For a few minutes he closed his eyes and concentrated on the smells of wood, dust, and idle cellar space. He even mistakenly convinced himself that he'd been able to distinguish the perfumes of creams and ointments coming from the dressing room.

That effort carried him to Blanca, and he recognized in the thought of her a mix of fragility and majestic strength. That woman possessed a spare and savage essence that shredded all pretexts. One after another.

The show started, Santina D'Offerta performed for the two of them alone. And she was good.

Liguori had a series of lapses in concentration, he failed to take in the entirety of the monologue. Santina was barefoot, and her feet were petite and vibrant. Her hair was long, unruly, and as she moved, it revealed sections of shoulders and rapidly framed the slender swelling of breasts, only to cover them again, stirring expectations.

In the end, to avoid offending her with the applause of a mere four hands, Liguori stopped his friend from clapping and stood up to bow.

Carolina smiled.

"I get it, I'll introduce you to Santina and leave the rest to the two of you."

Liguori hurried through a summary courtship, had dinner with the actress, and accompanied her back to the hotel.

He found a strongly detached pleasure with her. As he was putting his clothes on, he thought about Blanca.

21.

Once the girls left the apartment Blanca got into the shower. She kept the faucet at the lowest level, she was happy with a weak dribble of water. Her skin had become a veil that could be torn by importunities that were a trifle to others.

As she got ready to go out, she thought of what Tita had said: once again she had met a girl who'd been forced to grow up too quickly, to confront fears for which her emotional reflexes were unprepared.

A ferocious vigilance swelled within her for her own life, that of her daughter, and for those who had not been afforded the rare privilege of growing up with all appropriate slowness.

Sergio led her on foot to the Fuorigrotta police station, which was only a short walk away.

Blanca gave him the rest of the morning off; she'd ask Malanò permission for an inspection and then she'd have a cop accompany her to the San Paolo Stadium.

"If I need you, I'll call you, I don't know if I'll have to go to Pozzuoli afterward."

"So this thing you have where you bark out orders, does it all come from your dog-training years?"

"I doubt it. Dogs are sufficiently blind that they instinctively recognize what is wanted of them by those they love. See you later."

A policeman showed her to the waiting room outside Malanò's office.

After the first half hour in the waiting room she began to grow impatient. There was lots of activity, people coming and going, slamming of doors, hasty agitated footsteps, alarmed voices interrupting each other.

The whispered snatches of conversation she caught as people hurried past told her that something big had happened.

After an hour, she decided that she had waited well beyond the limits of decency. She got up and went in search of the buzz of voices that might have offered her some explanation of all that hubbub. She moved with uncertain steps, since she didn't know the place and the confusion and racket wasn't helping her to identify the spaces she needed to traverse.

She was getting annoyed.

She stopped to take a few deep breaths, her usual instinct for movement simply didn't work if compromised by agitation.

She headed for the door to Malanò's office. She couldn't stand there eavesdropping, so she followed the perimeter of the wall. With light finger taps she managed to find a place where the wall was a little thinner. She could even move away from the wall and pretend she wasn't doing a thing, the sounds from inside would reach her anyway.

Three different voices came from the room. She managed to isolate herself from the noise and focused on the words that came out of Malanò's office. The voices blended, interrupting each other, in excitement. There were only a few comprehensible words: *serial*, *again*, *Verona*, *poison*.

That was all she needed.

She gave in to another wave of fury, which she channeled into a powerful, quick-acting, concentrated violence. Then she halted it. She needed a clear mind.

She had no more time to waste.

She went back to the door, felt around for the handle so she could go in.

A police officer standing guard blocked her way. Blanca turned her head and lowered her voice, putting a sense of power into it that the cop hardly expected.

"You would be well advised to let me through."

The man stepped aside.

When she made her entrance, the three men stopped talking. Blanca reached around for a chair and sat down.

"I'm guessing that the murder of Julia Marin is linked to the death of Vialdi."

"Who are you? Who let you in here?"

"*Buon giorno*, Captain Malanò, I'm Sergeant Blanca Occhiuzzi, from the Pozzuoli police station. If I'm not mistaken, you actually requested our help. Tell me about the murder. By the way, I met with Julia Marin just a few hours ago, at your request."

"Who gave you this information?"

"The wall."

"That's a joke in questionable taste."

"Where? Where was the corpse discovered?"

Malanò's instinct for secrecy and dislike for this woman were overwhelmed by his pleasure in being able to confirm to her the seriality of the murders.

"Bentegodi Stadium. The corpse was found with legs spread-eagled, back bent against one of the goalposts, face turned toward the back of the net. Clenched in her teeth was a blade of grass from the soccer field. I'll be the one to decide when and if I wish to receive information about your interview with the victim, right now I have more important things to think about. I'd really like to see anyone dare claim that my hypothesis about the serial killer is groundless."

"Is there some prize at stake?" Blanca flashed a sad smile and thought about Tita's mother and her daughter's fears.

"Sergeant Occhiuzzi," Malanò uttered Blanca's surname as if it were a threat, "you can go and report to your superior officer. Good day."

Blanca remained seated and requested an officer to accompany her to the stadium for an inspection.

"There's nothing to be seen at the San Paolo Stadium, and the man who found Vialdi's corpse has already been amply questioned."

"Even if there was anything to see, I wouldn't be the right person. I'm legally blind, my specialty has to do with wiretaps and environmental listening devices."

Malanò pretended to be embarrassed, though that was hardly the case. All he wanted was to get Blanca out of his hair.

"My apologies. So why do you want to go there?"

"Captain, you are following your own theory. Everybody has one. You may not believe me, but my blind theories work remarkably well. So, are you going to give me an escort?"

22.

What passes is love, thrill, the frenzy of the last instants. What passes is the certainty that I can stop you, hold you, finally have you all for myself.

It passes.

The hunger has returned, I wish I could kill you all over again.

Nothing to be done about that. I don't get encores. Death has already made your acquaintance: your head lolling, the slight jerk, the definitive slumber, on a well established scholastic schedule, the tiny, inoffensive hole in the center of the mole. And they say that murderers lack a sense of humor: I'm laughing, can't you see? I'm laughing.

Perhaps the end I provided was defective, a gunshot fired with a blank, a magic trick performed with the tattered shreds of a rabbit that resuscitates before my eyes.

And yet for a while your death had placated me, you know that? Even a sense of guilt came around asking after me. Not the guilt you're thinking of, no. The remorse that I hadn't kept you alive, but deprived of consciousness. I could have done it, too: I have an impressive mastery of pharmaceuticals.

I'd be capable of dosing an absence of hydrocortisone.

I'd be capable of artificially increasing the prolactin supply to the bloodstream.

I could hold tyrannical dominion over target cells.

I'd be capable of overwhelming even the autocrine hormones that deactivate the very same nucleus that generated them.

I would be skillful at vivisecting your genitalia, slowing to a feeble trickle the gushing flow of testosterone that you once sprayed like a foul ointment over the requests of women, men, and of course your own demands. Continuous exhausting demands.

And in the end I would have been able to monitor the final and fatal stab wound into the hypothalamus, making your daughter tropines vanish into a burst of applause.

I needed much science, I needed much love to hate you to this point.

23

Rosina Mastriani headed down the street that she knew so well.

She'd lost weight, the cuts that she had inflicted were also intended to eliminate hunger and exhaustion. She looked around her: the sidewalks, the buildings, the vague mass of people, the buzzing, the colors, the rain, the sweet and salty odor, the cars had all lost their substance. As had she.

She turned toward the uphill lane where the girl lived, the narrow street was lined with porticoes and balconies, balustrades, shop signs, marble jewels, votive shrines that jutted out among the graffiti and the aging plaster. She counted the steps of the baroque church, someone had hung an umbrella from the bronze skull on the outdoor handrail.

These were her alleys and lanes, mockeries of life and death.

She caught herself repeating a childhood ritual: when she got to a certain point along the road she turned around. If she saw a shaft of sunlight toward the mouth of the road downhill, on the main thoroughfare, it meant everything would work out for the best. It was an innocuous superstition, a prediction. A little white lie of hope.

The people in the distance formed part of a chaotic army, which kept marching, marching toward her. A bit of sun fell and tangled the shapes in a bright blinding fog.

Rosina Mastriani drew strength from her private oracle and mastered a brisk, decisive stride.

She walked up steps, down alleys, and wended her way through and around closely parked cars. Her perception of the thinness of the buildings, windows, and loggias did not diminish.

It started raining again.

In the fall, sun and water joined hands and danced close; they whirled in alternation on the cornices of the buildings, glared indignantly at the undisciplined parabolas, the seventeenth-century ornaments offended by those borrowed from insolent displays of vanity, the window bars and walls. Sun and water paid no attention to where their consequences would be felt. They hung in suspension, tossing detritus down on the lives below them.

The woman took shelter from another downpour in a doorway: the concierge recognized her and seized her cheek between thumb and forefinger.

"It's you. What a long time it's been!"

Rosina replied no with a shake of her head: it wasn't her, not then, not now. She brushed aside the gesture that brought the years of another life back to her.

She ran away through the rain and went in search of her husband.

She reached the gambling den, as she called it. She saw the car. Now all she needed to do was wait. He wouldn't be coming out before three in the morning. At home with the children, she could be sure she'd find the witch of a thousand insults: Aunt Immacolata, her husband's wicked old relation.

She saw his car, picked up a rock, clutched it in her fist. It was music to her ears, the sound it made against the side of the car as she nonchalantly walked past.

She felt cold. She thought of going into one of those big stores, with air-conditioning, songs, dressing rooms where a person could sit, and escalators, but the streets with that kind of department store were so far away. She remembered of the time she took her infant son to the emergency room at the nearby Annunziata Hospital.

She reached the hospital and headed toward the seating in the waiting room.

The place was ideal, she too promised herself a cure and healing that might never actually come true.

It was mostly mothers with young children waiting for their turn to be seen. Rosina felt in a body-memory the sensation of her own children, as they moved in her womb, a womb that was so unready to house new life. She'd believed that in part she'd tamed her own sense of guilt for having abandoned them.

Her legs started shaking, she couldn't go on sitting there.

She walked out into the courtyard. A light that seemed to come from a flame poured out of a side door. She walked in and stood there breathless.

What had appeared from the outside to be just another ordinary cellar space was actually an enchanting jewel box: the space, a circular room with eight pairs of columns, was another belly. An ancient womb without sins or convulsions. Perhaps it had witnessed enough things to crucify them forever in the high vaulted ceiling of a grey sky, where the stars were amalgamated into curved lines, glued onto the galaxy of white plaster of centuries past.

She stood there, at the center of the circle, and tried out her voice. It came back to her as a remote, distorted sound, the sound of illness and wrongs archived over time.

The watchman told her that he'd have to be locking up. Rosina, stunned by the impression the place had made on her, told him that she didn't know where else she could wait. She didn't specify for what or whom. The man invited her to a ground-floor apartment in the Sanità quarter that he also used as an office. She went with him, and drank the hot milk and bread he blithely offered her.

She calmed down and listened to the man's stories: he knew everything about the Ruota degli Esposti, the foundling wheel or baby hatch where mothers abandoned unwanted children.

For the first time in months the thought took shape in her mind that she still might be able to offer something to her children, be it only the error of her ways, the sum of her mistakes.

When she got back to the gambling den her husband was just coming out. He had his arms around a girl.

She looked him in the eye.

"If you go on pitting my children against me, I'll report you to the police."

"Oh really? I'm so scared," and he climbed into the car with the girl next to him. Rosina put her hands on the hood of the car and didn't move.

The man laughed, put the car into first gear, and slowly began to move forward. Then he leaned out the window.

"Don't tempt me."

24.

After her inspection of the stadium, Blanca didn't feel like calling Sergio. And above all she had no wish to speak, she wanted to focus on organizing her thoughts about the morning's events without having to contend with music and words.

She asked the police officer who had taken her to the San Paolo Stadium to take her to the bus stop now.

The man hadn't given in for even an instant to the compassionate manners that Blanca so detested; he had also provided her with essential information that hadn't yet emerged from the Fuorigrotta police station. She thanked him.

"No, I thank you, Sergeant. I'm almost tempted to transfer over to where you work; but no, bosses come and go and our jobs stay right there."

Blanca boarded the bus, counted the stops, and got out in front of the Temple of Serapis. She followed the iron railing around the hollow of the Macellum.

She didn't want to hurry, her feet obeyed her, she felt safe.

She managed to rise from the depths with an impulse to climb. Her handhold gave her the necessary strength, she couldn't have done without it.

She thought of her sister, who died in the same fire that ruined her eyes.

"Look at me, you see me? I'm capable of being free again."

She looked over and down. From the bottom of the excavations the stagnant water wafted up a scent of a moss-lined well. She felt a giddy hint of vertigo, and the need to lift her head to breathe the salt air from the nearby sea.

Once again the flash of light. Powerful sunlight shattered the shadows and brought forth statues, columns, and shops.

An affectionate warmth rose from her stomach to her face; she felt her cheeks heating up and the course of her thoughts proceeding, with great precision.

She got to the police station and told Carità to ask Martusciello and Liguori to join her in her office. She had news.

The two men came in together just a short while later. Blanca turned a cool face to their wisecracks about the request for a house call.

She found determination and flat logic, laying to rest the issues attendant upon the presence of Liguori. The climb she'd just completed had a great deal to do with him as well. She began to recount in great detail the first part of the morning spent in the Fuorigrotta police station. Martusciello started pacing up and down in front of Blanca's desk.

"So Malanò told you that the interview with Julia Marin is less important than the other nonsense he has to attend to. We should have known he was going to clutch tight to that honorary second degree for his theory about the serial killer! What the hell does he care if we had a conversation with the victim just a few hours before someone murdered her?"

"What an idiot," Liguori piped in, comfortably seated in his chair. "So he didn't even find out that, on account of it being lunchtime, we decided to question Julia Marin together with Mara Scacchi."

"Liguori, this isn't the right time. Go be a knight in shining armor without a horse somewhere else."

Blanca went on as if neither of the two men had spoken.

"Afterward, I had an officer accompany me to the stadium. I wasn't looking for anything, but . . . "

Liguori spoke in a detestable tone of voice over his half smile.

"Sure though, the impressions, the voices, the traces of lingering thoughts, and all that sort of thing."

Blanca went on ignoring him.

"It was a good thing I went to the stadium. We ran into a great many members of the security staff, and okay, this may be a normal thing after a murder, but I did find it odd that normal operations would call for only one guard on duty. I expressed my doubts to the police officer, and he told me that the guy who found Vialdi's body was not only the only security guard present that night, but is also apparently in close contact with the families involved in the soccer betting rings."

Martusciello could hardly contain himself:

"I'm going to talk to him."

Liguori, too, got to his feet:

"On the other hand, Captain, Blanca and I are going to Verona."

"To do what?"

"Oh, I don't know, impressions, voices, traces of lingering thoughts, and all that sort of thing."

"Do whatever you like. I have no time to argue with you. You can only stay away three days, though, we've got work to do here."

Blanca said nothing, her newfound strength had just taken one more shove toward the sea floor.

25.

Martusciello went to the taxi stand down by the harbor. He was uneasy, he didn't want to waste any time. Julia Marin's murder was on the short list of his mistakes.

The first cabbie in the line waved for him to get in, but the captain was searching for a driver he knew personally: Viciè Morbide, or according to his license—Vincenzo Coppola.

Viciè Morbide had won his nickname on the field, or actually, on the sea, because he'd been able to buy his own taxi thanks to years and years of smuggling soft pack cigarettes—*morbide*, as they were known in Italian—covering the sales territory from Pallonetto to Santa Lucia.

"Captain, what an honor. Are all your regular squad cars in for repairs?"

"They're fine, but out of gas. Take me to the stadium. Then wait for me outside."

"They threw quite a party for Vialdi!"

"What's the word on the street, Viciè?"

"I can't be of any help to you, I'm sorry. In fact, I'm happy to say it: my network isn't *the* network, and you know that." Viciè Morbide parked his white Fiat Punto outside the players' entrance.

A security guard stopped Martusciello. The captain sat down on a low wall, told the guard he had all day, and finally wore him out by relentlessly demanding information about the night watchman who had been the first to stumble on Vialdi's corpse.

"Let's just say that Gioacchino Rizzo has taken up residence inside the plant."

"Inside the ex-Italsider steel mill?"

"He used to have an apartment in Bagnoli, but then his wife tossed him out because he's always drunk. He got in touch with the Chinese who were disassembling the steel mill piece by piece, they left him a sort of shed that was part of the old infirmary. Which they didn't want anyway, they're just looking for the steel and iron that they can sell to us. Asbestos is no good to them. That's where Gioacchino is. Do me a favor and don't tell him that you found out from me, I wouldn't have said a word except that you were so relentless. Wait, are you really a mail carrier?"

"Look at my shoes: instead of a size they have zip codes."

"If you manage to find Gioacchino, tell him that if he doesn't go to work they're going to fire him. He can say that he's still in shock all he wants, but sooner or later . . . "

"I'll let him know."

The captain went back to the taxi and asked Viciè Morbide to take him to the plant, taking the road that led through Posillipo. When they reached the crest of Coroglio Hill, he told him to pull over: he got out and surveyed the area from above. He wanted to identify the most isolated entrance.

An expanse of land left the surviving bastions of what had once been a mighty steel mill isolated.

Once again, Martusciello marveled at the surviving, repurposed beauty: Naples was still a mermaid at a ripe old age, beautiful, teeth clenched down on the silver hook, while the pirates sawed away at the still living tail, glistening with scales and blood.

The island of the blast furnace incarnated a crucifixion of the sea, the land, and a piece of the history of a quarter that had once vaunted its dignity.

He selected the most discreet entry point.

"If you don't see me come back, call the Pozzuoli police station and alert Liguori or Occhiuzzi. Write down this number."

"Captain, if I don't see you come back . . . easy to say, but you take a long time to do things. Do you still keep your gun unloaded?"

"Yes."

"Good, that sets my mind at rest."

As soon as Martusciello ventured into the abandoned area, his point of view changed; a wall worn away by iron dust isolated the zone at a certain distance from sea and buildings.

The spirals of barren dirt and scrub led the captain into a landscape befitting a ghost town, thoroughly picked over in the aftermath of the ransacking for precious metals.

Still, his feet had become obedient once again, and he had a renewed, pioneering patience. At least for the moment.

From a distance he recognized the infirmary grounds, long ago he'd met a young Carmine Grimaldi there for work at the beginning of his career—at the time he was a substitute physician.

The sheet metal door of the surviving section of industrial shed wasn't heavy, and the gentle breeze banged it against its housings.

He went in, but found that he was disturbing the rats that were grazing on the corpse of Gioacchino Rizzo.

He walked out to keep from vomiting. Whoever said that the eyes get used to certain sights? He picked up a fallen branch and pounded on the sheet metal from outside. The rats scattered, snouts and paws stained with a faded red.

The captain tried to work up the courage to go back into the shed. He stalled, taking a great many more minutes than he was able to count. In the meanwhile he kept pounding the branch against the sheet metal, against death, and against the line of work that had been stitched to his back from birth like a shirt of misfortune.

The echoing sounds of the old steel mill brought back blast furnace flames which seized at his throat.

He managed to go back in after thoroughly cursing the misery and pain of that sense of duty of his that would never allow him to simply turn his eyes away.

The rats' teeth were unable to conceal the cause of death, a bullet hole was still visible on one of his temples, gray matter had spattered the corrugated sheet metal walls.

The pounded dirt floor was strewn with the glass from broken bottles. Martusciello hoped that Rizzo had had a chance to drain them all dry before dying.

"Fixing, always fixing. I keep at it. I'm still here letting my head invoke another hodgepodge of corrections in the midst of all this filth." He walked back out into the open air.

He fell to the ground there where he stood. A shrill whistle reached his ears and the grey of the steel evaporated into his eyes. His spongy limestone heart gathered a new burst of urgency to leave and his heartbeat set out to run in obedience to that impulse.

The sound of a siren did nothing to distract his attention from his surrender.

Liguori and Blanca got out of the car. Viciè Morbide had decided that he'd waited long enough even considering Martusciello's sense of time.

The detective inspected the shed, called the forensics team, and alerted Captain Malanò.

Blanca reached out for Martusciello's hands and helped him to his feet. She'd found him sitting on the ground, his back resting against sheet metal.

"Are you all right?"

"I need to go home. I want to wash up."

26

The next day a heavy silence descended over the Pozzuoli police station. But the excitement only increased in the Fuorigrotta police station.

Malanò organized a press conference and drew up a semi-official list of the journalists who were welcome, making it clear that he'd already cleared that list with the chief of police.

With the confidence of one who had guessed the past, present, and future he placed a telephone call to Captain Adami of Verona, inviting him to *join forces* with him in a *productive working alliance.*

"*Buon giorno*, colleague, this is Rosario Malanò from the Fuorigrotta police station, Naples. I've already had an opportunity to converse with one of your detectives, Francesco Coppola, a fellow southerner, but I'd prefer to speak directly with you."

"Francesco reported to me, sorry, but as you can imagine, I'm swamped on account of recent events with which you're no doubt familiar."

"Yes, I can imagine. You must work hard up there."

"Naw, not really. It's a quiet province we live in."

"No, perhaps you don't follow me, Adami, I meant you work hard in general." Adami continued not to follow him. "Anyway, as soon as this storm, both media storm and otherwise, passes—because the journalists are jumping around like crazy here—I'll come see you for a conversation about this very interesting case."

"If you can't come up, I'll be glad to send you any and all useful documents. We are expecting the autopsy results."

"Yes, we're waiting for the results on Vialdi's death too. But you know how things are down here: I'll bet that your results come in before ours do."

"I wouldn't be so sure."

"Thanks, Adami, courteous as always. Talk to you again soon."

"Talk to you soon."

As soon as he hung up the phone, Malanò felt the need to inform someone sitting in his office of the differences in levels of professional skills to be found in the north and south of Italy.

Detective Liguori pestered chorus girls, criminals, recording technicians, costume makers, impresarios, dancers, dealers, waiters, and a considerable number of other people who had crossed paths with Vialdi. After each conversation, which the detective always managed to pass off as a chance encounter, he jotted down in his smartphone every word spoken, every impression received. In the end he noted: "No recording of last concert."

He was looking for something new but he continued not to find it, everyone confirmed more or less mechanically a picture of a personality and habits that Vialdi hadn't bothered to conceal. He saw an order of circumstances and impressions far too emphatic for his tastes. The confirmation of a serial killer at work in the midst of a complicated life, according to script, struck him as a signature in block letters, clearly legible and therefore completely odious.

Blanca waited for Nini in the kitchen, standing and eating her breakfast. She told her that she'd overheard them talking about Tita's fears and that unfortunately they couldn't be ignored, especially after the murder of one of Vialdi's lovers and the killing of the night watchman who had found the man's body in the stadium. She wanted to talk to the girl's mother.

"If Tita finds out about my meeting with her mother, tell her that I heard the two of you talking, and you're free to blame me for being nosy. Don't alarm her past a certain point, but explain to her that I had no choice but to question her mother. Inform her that this is a legally required procedure."

"She'll hate me."

"Probably so. I'll have to go to Verona, I'll ask Sergio to come keep you company."

"I don't need a babysitter. I'm grown up now, I'm fifteen years old."

Blanca lowered her voice in the forceful tone that Nini knew all too well.

"I didn't ask your opinion and I know how old you are."

Nini made one last stab by adopting a conciliatory tone of voice. But no was still no.

After a night spent pacing back and forth on his balcony, Martusciello shaved with the bathroom door open, listening with one ear to the morning television news. The irritating words had broken out of their cages.

One special explored in depth the history of serial killers in Italy:

The case of the Neapolitan serial murderer . . .

No doubt, they're showing a montage with a photo of him and his certificate of residence.

. . . offers one striking geographic fact: up till now the phenomenon of serial killers has been almost entirely unknown in southern Italy; the comparable cases, of which half have been brilliantly solved, occurred in northern localities.

"Northern localities. What is this guy, a real esate agent?"

Advanced industrialization and prosperity, according to the psychiatrist Dr. Di Buni, tend to encourage aspirations to necro-mania in developed societies.

"What developed societies? Developed into open sewers, is what they are. You've all lost. You understand that, don't you? Progress has been nothing but a con job, an illusion of wealth. Assholes. Them and us both. And so we're becoming emancipated in the south, we even have our own Bocconi business schools. Degrees in murder. As if our own native industries weren't enough."

Now let's move on to an examination of the suggestive position, clearly sexual in nature and intent, in which the dead body of one of Jerry Vialdi's lovers was found; Vialdi, a popular neomelodic recording artist, was also found dead . . .

"Santina, would you shut that damned thing off! Hell's bells and dead slut bodies! There they are, rats like yesterday's, scurrying around unearthing rotten scabs."

Santina turned down the sound and stuck her head in the bathroom door.

"They're just chasing after ratings. That's the way it works. Just thank your lucky stars they didn't broadcast the pictures, the way they did with the latest murdered dictator."

"Hmmph, this detached attitude of yours, scholar that you are, with your finger marking your place in the book, is enough to shatter my nerves."

"And for me your shattered nerves just bring me back into an acceptable state of normality. Ever since the operation you haven't . . . "

"I don't want to talk about it and you know it. I'm leaving."

Santina waved farewell to her husband with relief and with equal relief greeted solitude and the new day.

27

Tita lived at the bottom of the long road running toward
Coroglio. Blanca asked Sergio to describe the view from
the panoramic road to her.

The smell of the sea and the impending business trip with
Liguori demanded a reliable external space, scanned by fully
functional eyes. Blanca wanted to escape her own senses, far
too partisan at that crucial moment.

For years her work in Liège, Belgium, had made her com-
petent, unfettered, and quite undomesticated. She earned her
daily bread by concealing her difficulties. She'd never been
interested in complaints, explanations, warnings. She preferred to turn her back and head elsewhere.

Since Nini had come to live with her, she'd had to do without that particular resource. In Pozzuoli, she did more than
just work with wiretaps and listening devices, and her daily
interactions with Martusciello and her other coworkers kept
her from fleeing across the moats of isolation.

The return to Naples had blown solitude sky high: it had
crumbled into rubble and the detritus had left accessible pas-
sageways.

"Maybe that's why love has begun to infiltrate," Blanca
mused, then turned to Sergio: "What can you see from here?
Tell me."

"And what can I tell you? The blue sea, the sun, boats, terraces, pine trees, villas with views of Capri, and lots of traffic."
Blanca wondered if she too would get so used to the sight of

the sea, the precision of the hues, the laziness of being able to squander pictures, taking only the part you wanted and discarding the rest with a haphazard blink of the eye. She didn't know how to answer.

She was afraid that the capricious flash would pay her another visit, but this time the epiphany of light left her in peace.

"I'm Sergeant Blanca Occhiuzzi."

"Please, come right in, I'm Maria Datri, I'm Tita's mother." A bright shadow projected from the far side of the room, there must be a glass wall or a wide French door.

From the kitchen came the clatter of pots and pans, the smell of onions and oil.

"My apologies for the timing."

"I prefer it this way; Tita isn't home from school yet."

Blanca explained that she had to meet her: she considered Julia Marin's murder a grave oversight on the part of the investigating detectives, and therefore on her own part as well.

She expected reluctance, but instead Tita's mother unleashed a flow of words.

"I knew Julia Marin. When she came to Naples I'd spy on them. They'd go off to stay in a hotel in Mergellina, and I'd sit in my car out front until Jerry came out and went home. He knew I was there, and once he even waved to me from a distance. He was laughing. His shirt was all rumpled and untucked and his eyes looked younger. It was clear that he was happy when he was with her. Julia Marin wasn't like me, she never objected to anything. I followed her right before her death. She was beautiful. I watched her board the train, her and her goddamned calmness. I envy her. Even though she's dead I envy her. The lunatic who murdered them united them. You may be thinking I'm a mother with a daughter, that the things I'm saying are scandalous and so on and so forth. There's nothing I can do about it."

"Vialdi was a person who . . . "

"Definitions are no use to me, please don't try. What Vialdi had was the ability to go to people in their nothingness and take them somewhere far away. That was his skill. And maybe that was because he knew it so well, nothingness. Would you say no if someone offered you a chance to wake up for just a few hours after years and years of wandering in a daze?"

Blanca thought of Liguori and Nini: maybe she should try to find some excuse to avoid the trip to Verona.

"Tell me about the singer's love of gambling."

"He racked up debt, he enjoyed losing everything he had. I don't know if it was because he loved starting over, or if he was trying to intimidate even himself. He turned to the same dealer to make bets and for cocaine."

"Who was that?"

"I don't know the name of the lawyer, which is what he always called him, but if I did I'd tell you. All I know is that when I was in Pozzuoli he'd send me away whenever he needed to see him. The lawyer always came to his place. Jerry liked, I don't know exactly how to put this, but Jerry liked being on edge."

"Did the lawyer know about you?"

"About me, you're asking?" Blanca nodded. "Of course he knew, everyone knew about me and Jerry." Maria Datri picked a handful of ornamental stones from a bowl and started handling them uneasily.

"Even your husband?"

"Yes. It was the only good thing that I ever managed to do for Tita. I stayed and I let my husband play the part of the good guy, but I hope you'll understand if I prefer not to talk about all that."

Blanca shifted her shadowed gaze away from the direction of the woman's voice. Before going away she wanted to fix in her mind the variation of tones in the woman's words.

To Maria Datri it seemed as if the police sergeant were staring at a painting on the facing wall.

"It's a Medusa head by a nineteenth-century imitator. This Medusa's gaze is false, it wouldn't turn anyone who looked at it into stone."

"I was never in any danger."

After Blanca left, Maria Datri's husband joined her in the living room:

"My compliments for the thorough confession. Did she absolve you? Lunch is ready."

"Wait for Tita and eat with her. I'm not hungry."

28

Blanca called Martusciello and told him about the meeting. The captain focused with special attention on what Maria Datri had confided to her about the lawyer.

"I don't have anything specific. I can't help you there," Blanca said.

"Okay, for starters I'll ask Marialuigia Moreno, maybe she knows something."

After giving a faithful account, the sergeant added the impressions she'd taken from the questioning session. She didn't bother about logic, and the captain was glad to indulge her, in fact he welcomed her lack of precision.

By the time Martusciello realized that an insignificant drizzle had accompanied him on his walk, he was already drenched.

When he looked up, he saw that the plants on Vialdi's terrace had a general appearance of disorderly neglect. He wasn't sorry to see it.

The horizon line of the sea was close in and grey. An expanse of sheet metal.

He was overcome by a fit of agitation; it had taken the place of indolence ever since he'd found the night watchman's body.

At night, his heart kept him awake. It demanded attention with the perpetual motion of obsession, pounding the kettledrum of heartbeats.

The summertime line for the swing had became a race through gray fog.

The captain rang Marialuigia Moreno's buzzer, and in a very short time, she was downstairs in the street.

"Let's drive. Sorry if I didn't invite you to come up."

"I won't take up much of your time. Did you know that someone murdered Julia Marin?"

Marialuigia Moreno started the engine and pulled out, heading toward Pozzuoli. The rain started falling harder, Martusciello's wet clothes contributed to the misty patina spreading on the interior of the glass.

"I didn't find out until last night."

"Did you know her?"

"Not very well, just like I didn't know any of the others very well. I'm not taking anyone's side here, but it seems understandable to me that a successful man, with plenty of interaction with the public, should be a frequent and inclusive dater. Vialdi made no promises of emotional stability and that was not something he was looking for. I'm positive about that. I think it's about time we stopped investigating the sexual habits of consenting adults of any kind."

"You can't breathe in here." Martusciello rolled down his window. "We need to investigate and certainly not out of any delight we might take in chastising the lustful, but because there's a murderer at work, and one who takes a certain delight in the theatrical. As far as that goes, I don't have a lot of experience: I still love, after all these years, the same woman. Only, I guess, not as well as I once did, perhaps with longer silences and with a temperament that seems determined to get worse with the passage of time. It's something that happens."

Marialuigia Moreno smiled at the unexpected confidence he'd just made. It was better suited to a more simple, sentimental place. She'd have liked a routine, even a boring one; she'd have preferred it to the words, the concerts, and the adrenaline that was hardly hers anyway.

Martusciello changed his tone of voice, feeling awkward about the confidence he'd made, unexpected even to him.

"Who is the drug dealer Jerry Vialdi referred to as 'the lawyer'?"

Awkwardness made him set his foot wrong. Generally the captain came to the point after a long time spent beating around the bush.

In fact, Marialuigia Moreno stiffened.

"And who told you that Jerry had a dealer?"

"He had one all right. You yourself confirmed that the Singing Maestro made use of controlled substances . . . "

"He never had to go buy them, Captain, he enjoyed home delivery, just like with the women he dated. That's all."

"That's all," Martusciello repeated, remembering that the first time they met Marialuigia Moreno had also shut herself up behind a *That's all*. "You're true to your words."

"Yes, to my words."

29

Martusciello headed for the subway station. A man was buying an umbrella from a street vendor:

"Don't you have one that's black?"

"Dottore, it's raining here and the fact itself is dark enough, why don't you take this one with a bright pattern?"

"Because it's horrible. That's exactly why we've lost everything we've lost: instead of concealing the ugliest things we put them on display. The years we still haven't emerged from teach us all the wrong things, and intentionally so, for ideological reasons. Even misdeeds used to dress themselves up better than they do now."

"Do you want the umbrella or don't you?"

"I'd rather get drenched."

Martusciello stepped closer:

"Liguori, must you even make life harder for poor street vendors?"

"Captain, what a pleasure, if I'd only known you were here I'd have redirected my energy to making life harder for you."

"You could pretend you never saw me. Ciao. I was just leaving."

"Me too. I dropped by the office, and now I'm going to pay a call on your good friend Malanò, and then back to the RAI. It seems odd to me that there's not a trace of Vialdi's last concert."

"Clearly, they're just trying to conceal the ugliest things instead of putting them on display. Liguori, don't indulge his mania for serial killers."

"I practically never indulge anyone, but you have to admit that the second murder confirmed Malanò's mania. I know, it's irritating for you." The captain looked off in another direction. "It irritates you, right? In any case, once Blanca and I get to Verona we'll be able to provide you with useful information about the Marin murder too."

Martusciello hunted through his pockets for his lighter. He tumbled it through his fingers before striking a flame.

"It won't do a bit of good to go to Verona, but I have more important things to discuss with you: has it occurred to you just how little the death of Gioacchino Rizzo, the stadium custodian, smacks of a serial killer? A nice clean kill, leaving aside the disgusting aspects of rats and general despair. Not a clue: forensics reports that a professional killer covered both shoes and hands. A precise, rapid piece of work, 9 mm. The kingpins around here seem to prefer foreign weapons, therefore the signature is even more credible. They added in bloody handwriting: we didn't do this."

"Captain, you're drawing patterns that are harder on the eyes than even that ugly umbrella."

The two men descended to opposite platforms. The subway train for Fuorigrotta came by a short while later. Liguori waved at Martusciello through the window, pretending to tip the hat he wasn't wearing.

The captain, in his turn, pretended that from where he was standing it was impossible to see into the subway car.

He knew perfectly well that Julia Marin's murder confirmed Malanò's theory, but hearing it from Liguori only increased the urgency to find the drug-dealing lawyer and other, less ready-made clues. He left the station, bought the umbrella at which Liguori had turned up his nose, and went in search of Funicella Corta.

He climbed Via Solfatara and at a crossroads headed off down the hardscrabble slope that the rain had turned into mud.

The fumaroles high above amused themselves by staging a dress rehearsal that spattered the territory below with water instead of lava. The rain smelled of sulphur and exhaust fumes.

A recently installed heavy iron door blocked entry to the farmhouse where the informant's family lived.

A woman came to the door and informed the captain that her brother had left. She didn't know where he'd gone.

"I'm supposed to tell you that when he comes home he's going to come see you and that the shambles inside the stadium was not the only one."

30

Blanca was packing to leave for Verona. Generally it was something she did well ahead of time. Generally, while she was packing her clothes, recognizing the fabrics by touch, the desire to stay home surged within her.

What became indispensable was the return home at the end of each day, eating without any regard for restraint, classical music against the racket of the day, the smell of her little patch of quiet, the disorderly sleep that was suddenly broken to find her free, and alone.

She mused that this time she wouldn't be able to give up her relative degree of autonomy. More than the other times. Three days with Liguori would mean little relief and the constant tension of making up for shortcomings.

Relative degree of autonomy, good one. Yes, yes, that was nice: a manifesto of shortcomings. This time I can't do it, more than at other times in the past. I'm tempted not to go at all, Blanca concluded, as she slipped into the suitcase her light dressing gown, the one that made her skin feel so smooth.

She heard the front door open and walked toward the sound. Nini asked forgiveness in a low voice as she greeted her with a kiss. She was with Tita, who started in with a harsh indictment.

"I just dropped by to thank you for the state of war now in place where I have to live. Not that there wasn't warfare before, but now it's even better! The disgusting mist of resentment and words that are broken off whenever I walk into a room where those two geniuses have just finished ripping each other to shreds. My father's got it stuck in his mind that my Mamma's latest act of idiocy has now exposed us to physical danger, he says that the policewoman said it loud and clear, he says that you warned her. What the hell did you say to her? What could the two of you even know about it? You sit here chatting away in your tree house while dogs pee at the foot of the tree." Tita turned to go, reaching for the door handle.

Blanca reached out and held her hand, swallowed the agitation of departure and the uncertain promise that the light dressing gown carried with it.

"Calm down. Nini has nothing to do with any of this." She dropped her tone of voice to a lower register, without making it any more understanding. "I was listening to you. I was hidden. I had no choice but to warn your mother she might be in danger. If you want to go ahead and have it in for the rest of the world, be my guest, but don't kid yourself that it's going to make you feel any better. Just do what you want. The two of us know all about that and then some, so if you're looking for backs to whip in your righteous anger, do us a favor and go find them somewhere else."

Tita squinted.

"I don't want to live there anymore."

Blanca invited the girl to come stay with them for a while. She had to leave on a business trip, but Tita and Nini could stay there with Sergio. She offered to call her parents to ask permission.

"There's no need. The only good thing about the hellhole I live in is that they let me do whatever I want."

"Well, that's nice. Go home, get whatever you need. We'll wait for you here. Ah, the rules here are that you do your studying, you respect the schedules, and the residents of the apartment are presumed innocent until proven guilty. You can go now."

Blanca and Nini remained alone. The woman asked the girl to help her pack her bag.

The windows and walls in Blanca's bedroom were specially built, designed to be as soundproof as possible. Sounds penetrated anyway, but at least at an acceptable volume. When it was relatively quiet outside, as it was now, the woman could better distinguish the rustling and movements of those who were with her. She stretched out on the bed and concentrated on Nini as the girl moved from place to place, choosing her clothing, reminding her of the colors, and then folded and packed them into her suitcase.

"Thank you, I didn't want Tita to come talk to you, but I didn't really know how to get around it. That's the way she is, she gets angry, but then she gets over it."

"Even understanding needs to have its boundaries, Nini. If there are problems, let me know and I'll come straight home." Blanca laughed. "Maybe you should tell me anyway, so I can rush home from this demanding business trip." Nini pulled the silk nightgown out of the suitcase so she could fold it more neatly.

"Don't you like taking trips?"

"I like it and I don't like it, Nini, the way I feel about almost everything."

"So what do you like and just like, period?"

"Not much in the world: you, Mozart, the smell of bread, certain intelligent minds, parts of the work I do, parts of certain emotions. Come here." The girl dropped the dressing gown and walked over to the woman.

Blanca ran her fingers over Nini's face: she ran them over her hairline, the shape of her forehead, the gentle arch of her closed eyes, the gentle slope of her nose, the form of her smile, the slight asymmetry of her ears.

She told herself that she would be able to go away and return home, not everyone was given such a beautiful anchor.

31

Rosina Mastriani checked the want ads every morning. Obsessive hunting was the hundredth cut. Even before Vialdi, her days hadn't really been her own. She tenaciously monitored the hours of other people. Her children's, the hours of the man she'd married whom she now feared. She always felt she was under examination, she obeyed all requests with military precision, anytime she fell short she was filled with fear. The meticulousness she aspired to was impossible to attain, she chipped off pieces of her rigid will, far from any emotional sweetness.

She'd gradually been emptied of consciousness and surprise. She'd gotten her first taste of the future a few days after the birth of her first child. Her compulsive sobbing had first started while she was changing its diapers, on the changing table in the bathroom. The baby cried to attract attention and she had cried along with it, but without the same expectation.

She'd locked the door behind her, so that she couldn't be seen, and she'd gone over to the window.

A number of buildings cluttered up the horizon. A patch of ground, however, had still survived all the construction work. Rosina identified some apples scattered on the hay in the little clearing; they were ready to be placed in wooden crates and taken to market. In the future she told herself that those apples had saved her and her baby's lives.

The windows of the other buildings were holes, cells, niches.

The clotheslines were links. For some reason, there was no movement in the other houses, no distraction of people; there were no voices. The asphalt in the enclosed space between buildings rose toward her and bid her take a step out, told her it wasn't that hard to do, just one or two little steps, maybe with the baby in her arms. The laziness of her body suggested that it was impossible to make any effort, even to lift her baby, even to take a single step toward the courtyard. Her spine no longer had any structural integrity, her vertebrae were made of butter and the child's screams were a noise that didn't concern her.

She needed orderliness, or at least chronology. She asked her own will for help, but it was nowhere to be found.

She muddled up her years, months, and days, until she couldn't remember whether it was evening, afternoon, or morning. She couldn't connect events and she put spring after summer. Even her despair belonged to some body that wasn't her own. The razor was right there. To feel her arms, she decided to wound them.

She would have gone on to her wrists, if she hadn't noticed a man bent over, packing the apples into a crate. The sheer indecency of her imagination recognized on her fingers the smooth peel of apples. As if those were her hands down in the tiny field. She smelled the bitter scent of annurca apples and the heedless response of life itself took over.

She shook herself, the days promptly went back into place; she finished dressing her baby boy who had lain there all the while diaperless on the changing table. She concealed the cut, she dried her eyes, and she opened the bathroom door.

She glimpsed the eyes of the man she'd married, closed her own, and braced for the blow.

"Don't ever lock yourself in."

At the time of the second baby's birth, her husband was already spending practically no time at home. He devoted himself to gambling, betting, other women. Rosina knew that she ought to leave but she didn't know where to turn or how she could feed her children. The words of her middle school teacher often returned to her memory: "The first freedom is the freedom from want."

Maybe the teacher was having a hard time making ends meet too. Rosina clung to her school days, which she remembered as a wonderful time.

She left the Rione Sanità every morning and went off to the Art Institute at Oltremare. She liked everything about it: in her dense language of an adolescent girl, she left behind the history of burial and the fascination of the stones where she'd been born and gave herself up trustingly to the progress that art promised. Nothing was going to stop her; she was going to be able to change. She'd shaved her red hair into a boy's crew cut and felt she had the power to achieve anything. She learned with glee, and she was good.

When they told her that there was no money to attend university she went off to look for work in Rome. She found a furnished room in an apartment building nicely lodged at a distance from the city center. To get to the capital she traveled in the opposing direction every morning, from the glass boxes of progress she migrated on a daily basis back to the fascination of stones, a fascination which, however, roundly ignored her: her day was spent in a cellar that someone had decided to glorify with the name of kitchen, cooking meals for tourists. The place not only taught her the disgusting array of substances that it was possible to pass off for food, it also made her yearn again for her stones back home and the grimaces and sneers of life and death, the entrance to the Quarries, the Fontanelle cemetery, the catacombs and the basilicas, the early Christian art, but also the little corner store where she could settle her bill at the end of each month, the doctor who was willing to take an espresso at the bar in payment for an after-hours office visit, or her own language, the tongue that had nursed her, protected her, defended her.

She returned home. She disguised herself as a girl who'd never gone away. She took on a slovenly appearance, to a far greater degree than before she'd ever left for Rome, and adjusted the content to match the appearance. She wanted to be like all the other girls. She wanted to fit in, to disappear. She stopped shaving her hair and chose a nice cropped pageboy like a leper from the edge of town: she'd lost all and any ambitions to be considered a member of the tribe of artists. She took a job as a clerk in a shirt shop, and was paid in cash.

She was almost immediately recognized by the boy who would become a man, the man that she married.

She pretended to be a woman and an obedient wife, and then became one.

No question, an untamed and fiery part of her was still alive, but when it emerged into the open, despite all Rosina's training to rein it in, it was greeted with kicks and punches from her husband.

32.

Liguori passed by the sergeant's apartment building on his way to the Fuorigrotta police station.

He looked up at Blanca's balcony with stadium view: *The sweetest honey / Is loathsome in his own deliciousness / And in the taste confounds the appetite.* Ah, Juliet, feel free to empty over my head all the chamber pots of Verona. What poor taste, to travel to a cliché of love with murder as a pretext! It's not my style. But what is completely typical of me is that, try as I might to come up with something original, I still wind up smack in the middle of the most bestial commonplace. Bah. Far better to express offensive sentiments toward the outside world, and right now the most outside place on earth is none other than Malanò.

The detective stopped to watch a few officers of the Financial Police who'd stopped some ticket scalpers under the sign reading Upper Bleachers—Entrance—Gate 20.

Three men on scooters started off after meaningful glances with those who had been arrested, possibly to warn the others selling counterfeit bills. Among those arrested, Liguori recognized Nino Sparaco, who was a resident of Lucrino and a frequent if unwilling visitor to the Pozzuoli police station.

Contradictory signals are arriving. Maybe even Malanò looks up every so often and sees past the certain horizon of the serial killer. I'll keep this to myself, too, because it doesn't do Martusciello good to have any kind of confirmation: if he stops thinking of himself as the sole village donkey in history, he loses heart. He stops in his tracks. I'm doing it for his own good, the detective mused before walking into the police station. Malanò couldn't see him right away. The detective took advantage of the wait to ask around, dropping questions with the apathy of someone not really interested in the answers. He wanted to know how the captain had reacted to the death of Gioacchino Rizzo and he wanted to know before he saw him.

Malanò was very familiar with Liguori's reputation and part of him feared it. The detective came from a noble family that had failed to rise courageously to a position of leadership, but to make up for that had held on to the threads of the right connections with both hands, to that genteel reserve of caste and wealth that operates clandestinely, to the contrived elegance that strives to build up walls and the closed circle of selective, elitist knowledge.

Captain Malanò had no way of knowing that Liguori, in becoming a policeman, had replied no to his birthright: the only duke the detective cared about was thin and white and was a singer. He had taken with him the knowledge and tastes of his birth and had ventured down from Via Palizzi to mingle in the borderland of Mergellina between ghetto and salt water.

Liguori stubbornly insisted on examining the chain of events, trying to identify in the exasperation of impulses that leads to crimes a certain order he could impose on his own restlessness. At least partway.

Perhaps the comfort he'd experienced recently could be attributed to a sort of surrender, the amused glance that he cast in the direction of what remained in any case incomplete.

Malanò didn't know of this, and since he was tenaciously weak with those he judged to be strong, he welcomed Liguori into his office with an excessive cordiality.

"Detective Liguori, what a pleasure to see you again."

"Thanks," Liguori replied, staring at the captain's campero boots, verging on the yellow. The captain noticed the look before going to take a seat behind his desk.

"Sergeant Occhiuzzi came to see me." Malanò took care not to express his own opinion about Blanca. "How is she?"

"Of all our staff she's solved the greatest number of cases, so I'd imagine you'd be pleased to have her assistance. We're traveling to Verona together."

The captain's face lit up:

"I only just received the autopsy results from Adami, the captain in Verona who's in charge of the case. Perfect, precise, and very fast. Death by poisoning: a fatal blend of pentobarbital anesthetic, which is what veterinarians use."

"If I'm not mistaken, it was used recently for an execution in the United States, triggering outrage."

"Yes, they also use it in places where euthanasia is legal. In other words, it's a famous poison."

Liguori cracked his first half-smile of the meeting. "Right, I heard they plan to give it an Oscar."

Malanò laughed too loud and too long.

"I'm delighted to see that you and your assistant are going to gather useful evidence on the scene of the crime and to determine that the murders of both Vialdi and Marin are the work of the same serial killer. I understood it immediately, from the very first murder: who else would ever think of laying out a corpse like that?"

"I'm in perfect agreement with you, Captain, perfect. I'll do whatever you tell me to do, for that matter the request for collaboration came from you in the first place and we are here to follow your orders."

Malanò was gratified by Liguori's hypocritical admission.

"When the games are over I'll be delighted to have you working at my side in the new team."

The detective recoiled at the words that had just been bandied about and for the second time flashed his half-smile.

"Now tell me something, what obstacles still remain to a full and final understanding that both murders were the work of a single serial killer? I paid close attention to your press conference, and you left open a few doubts, minor ones, but still you left them open."

One of Malanò's shortcomings was that he was unwilling even to consider the possibility that not everyone was quite as eager as he was to make his way and climb the ladder of success. It never occurred to him that years ago Liguori had willingly left the places where he most wanted to arrive. So he took the bait.

"What can I tell you, I had no alternative! The first obstacle is Grimaldi, the medical examiner. He keeps repeating like a broken record that he found no traces of poison in Vialdi's body, and no bullets or knife wounds either. He insists that clinically speaking the singer died from a heart attack. You try and tell him that no one goes to wait for their massive heart attack crouched in a tangled soccer goal net with a mouthful of grass! He'll tell you that he doesn't give a damn, that it's my problem, that he's never falsified an autopsy report and that he's not about to start now. He says that the only courtesy he can do for me is to redo his initial clinical investigations, but I suspect he's just trying to waste my time, because this precision of his will only drag out the official delivery of the autopsy report. The other problem is Rizzo's murder. To my mind, the death of the night watchman has nothing to do with the other two murders, but the chief of police recommends I go easy on that angle. I might very well be right, but we have to be completely certain, because if a link of some kind emerges later we're going to look like complete assholes." Malanò opened his mouth in an enamel-whitened smile. "You know, by now everyone's attention is focused on these cases. We're on the front page of the paper every single day, on all the most popular news broadcasts, we even took away the top news slot from the garbage emergency!"

"Truly a notable achievement."

Liguori continued the conversation without even bothering to try to direct it, he'd found out what he needed to know.

While Malanò continued to burn with enthusiasm for his theory, a police officer entered the room and brought him some documents. He glanced at Liguori compassionately; the captain had spoken of nothing else for days now, and the people who had to spend time with him were heartily sick of it.

The detective took advantage of the interruption to get to his feet.

"Well, so long, Captain, I'd better let you get back to work."

"Don't be silly, this is standard routine, come back and see me anytime. We're going to do great things together." The officer glanced at Liguori, raised his eyebrows and pinched forehead and nose together into an expression that clearly said: *Thank me, brother, I just saved your life.*

Immediately outside the police station, the detective stretched his back and twisted his neck. He'd had a hard time maintaining his posture and his demeanor.

He phoned Martusciello.

"Captain, where are you?"

"Detective, what the hell does it matter to you?"

"If you're mean to me I'm going to hang up."

"Liguori, you know exactly what I think of you when you're dying to tell me something but you just want me to beg you. Go ahead, I have no time to waste."

"All right, I'll tell you, but only because I've looked

around and I can find no worse police captains to go to. Call Grimaldi—no, wait, even better, go pay him a visit."

"Why?"

"My charitable impulses aren't quite that strong. Find out why for yourself."

"Liguori, you wouldn't recognize a charitable impulse if it bit you in the ass. I heard they arrested Nino Sparaco, good buddy of Funicella Corta."

"Really? Well, what do you know."

33.

The passage of time had worsened the malaise that had come to him with his discovery in the shed.

"I'm becoming a pain in the neck," the captain mused. "Who knows where I get this inappropriate squeamishness from?"

Before going into the morgue, he stopped to smoke in the open air. A breeze had sprung up and the palm tree standing guard outside the anodized aluminum entrance was trembling with the change in the weather and the chewing of the red palm weevil. The parasite was attracted in particular by damaged trees and it laid its eggs in existing cuts in the trunk and the fronds. There it ate its fill and awaited its metamorphosis. No cure seemed possible

The captain looked around and considered how the structure had deteriorated: the questions asked by surviving family members in flat, bewildered voices; the medicinal smells that refused to be confined by mere walls.

The parasite was not alone in its gnawing away at life.

Dr. Grimaldi was talking with a few of his colleagues. He saw Martusciello and came over.

"My how you've aged, Captain."

"And a very fine day to you too. Tell me about Vialdi." The doctor stipulated conditions: what he had to say was confidential. Malanò was pressuring him to have the results, but he still needed time to do some further exams and studies. He'd provide hypotheses only to certain cops, the ones who wouldn't insist on dictating the words he wrote.

"Tell me, but let's step outside, I need a cigarette."

"Hadn't you quit? Hold on, I'll get my own and we can go smoke outdoors."

The two men went off to a courtyard in the back that offered a panorama of closed windows, air-conditioning vents, and dangling cables: one electrical cable was preventing a shoe from completing its plunge to earth.

"So in Vialdi's body, I found traces of Lorazepam, a powerful sedative, and Propofol, a widely used anesthetic, intravenously injected. All the same, the levels of concentration of the drugs administered wouldn't be sufficient to explain the singer's death, which definitely was the result of a myocardial infarction. There is no doubt about that. In other words, the poison that Malanò is looking for, I was unable to find. Now, because it is unlikely, as our mutual acquaintance reminds me with suffocating frequency, that someone who is experiencing the first symptoms of a heart attack is going to choose *not* to hurry to the hospital and instead sneak into the stadium, crouch down in one of the goalposts, and start sucking on a blade of grass, I find myself in the position of having to search for something that is quite unwilling to be found. My first hypothesis is that someone injected a pharmaceutical that I just can't seem to identify. The second is that therefore a heart attack was simulated. The third is that only someone who knows their stuff would be capable of making such a complete fool of me."

"The number three is a genuine persecution. Forgive my simple village idiot ways, but couldn't it be that the killer simply was spared half the work by a weak heart? Vialdi must not have had a very sound ticker, cocaine'll do a number on you."

"Sure, maybe so, it's another theory, and perhaps the most likely one, but I don't include conjecture in my clinical reports. So let me get back to work."

"Not long ago I took a little excursion over to the old Italsider infirmary."

"I enjoyed working there. Memories embellish even asbestos."

34

Why so early? We could have moved at a more leisurely pace if we'd taken the train. I'm not sure if I brought everything with me. Is the hotel reserved?"

"Blanca, let's save the questions for the others. Let's just pretend we're two ordinary travelers. When are we going to have another chance to drop everything and go somewhere together for two nights?"

"And three days. Okay, Liguori."

"And today we don't have to work at all, that starts tomorrow. What do you want to listen to?"

"Mozart."

Liguori, Blanca, and Mozart left behind the industrial periphery of Naples and the traffic that went with it.

When Blanca recognized the highway from the smooth ride and the steady speed, she did her best to relax the muscles of her neck and admitted that she had no other excuses to turn back. Every so often she cracked the window and leaned her head into the breeze.

The vein in her right wrist pounded with the awareness of her eardrums. Since the night before, the woman had heightened the perception of every part of her body. She told herself that there were times when she could detect her own renal functionality, which had been accelerated recently, resulting in frequent trips to the restroom.

She focused on Mozart and sent him a silent prayer, a prayer that begged for peace with every beat of the vein in her right wrist.

In some way, Mozart responded and helped her to appreciate the quality of the sound and the absence of synthetic smells in the car.

Blanca caressed the upholstery of the car door. Liguori noticed the gesture and smiled.

"Can I change music, Signora? The next Requiem I hear, I'm going to drive under a semitrailer."

"Too bad for you if you can't appreciate someone who's capable of happiness even in the midst of death."

"I'm a simple soul, if there's one thing I like in life, it's happiness." He looked at her hands. "Especially lately."

After Rome, they stopped at an Autogrill. Blanca was beside herself, she didn't want to have to ask for help in moving around in a place she didn't known, but her agitation had begun to press down once again on bladder and kidneys.

With a level of intuition far greater than would have been expected, Liguori told her that he needed to go to the bathroom and led her up the steps with the discreet touch on her shoulder that the woman knew by heart.

The man's concern for her limitations surprised Blanca in the Autogrill bathroom. It occurred to Blanca that romantic moments were obliged to utilize what was at their disposal.

Amusement at the thought helped to break down the woman's defenses. It opened a breach in her capillary protection: blood reached her neck and stained it with an adolescent blush.

To the delight of the fates, in Blanca's memory that instant was bound up with the buzz of voices and the clatter of spoons and cups, the scent of bad coffee, thawed croissants, footsteps descending the stairs, and even the ringing of loose change in the attendant's bowl at the entrance to the bathrooms.

Liguori walked Blanca back to the car, and then asked her to wait for him.

In a short while, the man came back with a glass cup.

"I found the mint tea you like so much."

Blanca drank. She knew exactly how to savor a taste; she knew how to be entirely present both in her mouth and in the hot liquid.

"Good. How did you manage to find Lady Grey and fresh mint in an Autogrill?"

"All you have to do is ask. It's amazing how accustomed we are to asking a thousand things instead of the one thing we really want. What do you desire, Blanca?"

The woman said nothing, but just went on hungrily sipping her tea. In silence.

35

I t's no easy matter to be satisfied with the work you've done. No, no. With all the loving attention you can lavish on the most challenging project, carried out with total devotion, it can still be nullified by an unexpected flaw, an excess of contrivance or resentment.

Because you see, my dear Singing Maestro, the recipe demands a balance between good and evil. Sure, I know, you've infected me with meanness of spirit, phrases devoid of meaning, laws poised on the ordinariness of life. You tainted me with the shared pursuit of the least-worst.

The Least-Worst.

Acclaimed, pursued, without a thought for the fact that the least-worst does not even aspire to the supremacy of the final concluding roar.

Now then, pay close attention, or pretend to, since I can guess that you're not really all that interested. I wish to discuss issues of love and death:

A bite can be either a caress or an annoyance, the artistry is in gauging the pressure;

the administration of loving pain demands great precision in the doses prescribed, lest it spill over into the endangerment of life, otherwise the option of flight comes into play;

the roles of back and stiletto should occasionally be reversed; even in the most successful performances monotony lies in ambush like freshwater seaweed in a lake, wrapping around your ankle during a routine swim;

the murder of the philosophy of condescension is useful in the celebration thereof.

Above all, the aversion to freedom must itself come freely, and here I feel certain you fail to follow me. No enforced seclusion, no outright imprisonment can offer the sublime advantages of chosen captivity, of the unconditional offering of one's own neck to the fangs.

Maestro, and yet all this ethics of evil and passion was not enough to allow me to complete the task.
You well know it, and you laugh.
It is no consolation to me that uncompleted projects are in and of themselves an infinite calling.
It is no consolation.
I failed. And I can't try again. I haven't been a diligent boy. I've been a bad boy.

36.

In the hotel they checked into, Blanca couldn't hear the sound of the river. She called Liguori from her room: "Let's change hotels."

"As you please," the man replied. And it occurred to him that perhaps the rooms posed an obstacle or two too many. When they met downstairs in the lobby Blanca said that she wanted to look for a hotel somewhere near Ponte Pietra.

"No question, you have a way of barking out orders!"

"Julia Marin mentioned the sound of the river Adige. It strikes me as a waste not to be listening to it for the whole time I'm here."

"Don't you ever use the plural? Say, the first person plural, when you're conjugating a verb, for instance."

"For the whole time we're here."

"I like that better. At your service, Signora, let's leave the luggage here, I'll come back to get it once you've bestowed the grace of your decision on where we are to lodge for the night. Let's get going."

Liguori and Blanca walked to the middle of the Ponte Pietra. Standing in the middle of the bridge, the woman rubbed the instep of her foot against the back of her leg to stop the tingling from the cold.

"Tell me what you can see, Liguori."

"Here to one side we have a bicycle leaning against a trash can. The right toe clip and leather strap attached to the pedal are both more heavily battered than their counterparts on the left. This suggests that the bicyclist prefers to mount his bicycle from the right. The bicycle isn't locked, neither chain nor padlock is present: the owner is a trusting, lazy man. Behind the bicycle seat is a wicker basket, the kind that fishermen use. Wait." Liguori walked over to the basket, opened it, then came back to Blanca. "It's empty, so the bicyclist didn't catch anything: trusting, lazy, and unlucky."

"Ah, policemen! Now stop mocking the way I work."

"Do you want a more impassioned description? You have only to ask: pine trees like sighs striving upward, pitched roofs with red terra-cotta tiles, lovely colors: the white of stone, as untouchable as this heart of yours; sunset tinged with hues of pink and azure, colors that only nature can pair, let us confess, or else they become Jordan almonds in the window of a confectionery shop; transparent crystals of cold that melt against my youthful ardor. Do you like that better?"

"Youthful?"

"There, you doused my ardor. Now let's hear from the tour guide: in Verona you can admire the Torre dei Lamberti, the pale campanile of the Duomo, the city's cathedral, the church of San Giorgio with its majestic gardens and the smaller, but no less enchanting, Romanesque church of Santo Stefano."

"And the balcony?"

"No, I'm sorry, I can't take you to the balcony. Juliet is just itching to pour every goblet in Verona over my head. She says I'm too predictable, the fool."

"Predictable, I couldn't say, but you've certainly done a poor job of describing the world, good sir. Your youthful heart takes the benefit of seeing eyes with all the presumption of a world-weary habitué. By the way, do world-weary habitués eat dinner? If so, let's find a hotel, drop off our luggage, and go get something to eat." Liguori found a hotel overlooking the river Adige. Blanca went upstairs to her room and while she was waiting for Liguori to get back with the luggage, she took off her clothes and stood for a long time under the spray of hot water. She increased the water pressure and found to her surprise that it didn't bother her in the slightest. Probably the sound of the river distracted her skin.

The detective knocked on the door, Blanca clutched the collar of her dressing gown close to her neck.

"You need any help?"

"I can get dressed all by myself."

"But getting undressed, now . . . Really, though, you just beg the stupidest wisecracks, don't you?"

Liguori was enchanted at the sight of Blanca eating: from time to time she seemed to forget entirely that she was in the company of another person, and she showed that she was entirely alone with age-old movements of teeth and saliva. Then she'd regain her composure and be fully present again, sitting at the table, talking and laughing, only to wander off again into a flavor, into an indecipherable thought.

Blanca sniffed at her Amarone risotto with her nose a little too close to be seemly and felt a flush of shame. She shook her head and shoved away her sense of embarrassment, set down her fork, and picked up the solitary grape that sat in the middle of the dish: first she ate it with her fingers, squeezing it slightly to coax out a few drops of juice, then she lifted it to her mouth, holding it braced between her incisors before biting into it. Slowly.

"Can't you taste how good the bitterness is when it's paired with this slender sweetness?"

"You're turning mystical on me, Occhiuzzi."

"Who, me? Never been more flesh and blood in my life."

The man allowed himself to be dragged into a form of survival he'd never experienced before. Blanca clutched onto an excessive vitality, with her fingernails scratching the edge of the cliff, straining to experience the new, as if it were possible. Liguori abandoned his customary detachment and followed her.

He followed her courageously later, too, while they were making love.

37

Y ou won't stay?"
"See you tomorrow."
Blanca had gone back to her room and opened the door of the fridge crammed underneath the television set. It had taken her some time to locate it. The tiny bottles, all identical, gave her no information about what they contained. She'd opened one at random and set it down on the marble windowsill, where she'd taken a seat. The first sip told her that she'd selected a mixture of peach juice and rum. She didn't like it, but she drank it all the same. She wanted to drive away the strong taste of the two bodies twisted together, the ferocious striving for goodness and fear.

She started murmuring words, she needed to hear the sound of her own voice, she needed to tidy up her own mess.

The high heels I can never chance to wear be damned! I've been walking on stilts, blindfolded. What an idiot. And like a reckless fool running a risk she can't dare run, I even prayed: let the flash I can never control appear this time, let me see his face, and his hands, and his body, the color of his hair, the shape of his hips. Even if it isn't real, even if the light is imaginary. What good did it do, it was just wasted effort, I had to make do with the eyes in my fingertips. And I don't even know whether you realized. Or whether that was exactly why you wanted me. The exotic woman who lives in the world of blind shadows, instead, left afterward, didn't she, Liguori? She didn't stay there, adoring you, thanking you for the honor you'd just bestowed. What can I say, outsiders sometimes react with unexpected signals. Maybe you're sitting there thinking about it now, or else you just fluffed up your pillow and went to sleep. Satiated. But I'm not complaining, it's my fault that I don't know how to explain the sentiment that ranges from the cry *here we are: me, my terrible fears, the laborious exercise of my responses* to the decision to turn my back, keeping for myself a flat *if you don't understand that's certainly not my damned problem.* It's my fault up to a certain point, though: how could I tell you, Liguori, that I haven't been with a man for ten years? Ten years, that's almost how long you'd spend in prison on multiple charges of manslaughter. I wonder if you understood. You're so nice. You never left me alone for a moment, your body and your voice never stopped repeating to me *you see, we're the two of us, we're in the same darkness together.* After all, pitch darkness is what I insisted on, that much at least. You cheated: light came through a couple of loose slats in the wooden roller blind. I knew it immediately. *How did you know?* you asked me. Because you'd been a little too adept at reaching the bed without running into anything. But I didn't tell you. In fact, after you went back and closed the blinds properly, the way I wanted, the sound of your footsteps was hesitant, uncertain. The harmony of footsteps isn't something you learn in a minute's time. Just as it isn't easy for me to show you the body that I can't even see for myself. There, now we're even. I told you. And you got aroused in the presence of the mystery of my head. I wanted you, I couldn't wait any longer. In that moment it became clear to me that the story of some ordinary date, some hookup, wasn't something I could tell myself, so I set out with determination to take you back with me to Exoticland. *I could feign pleasure,* I thought to myself. *A displayed trembling and then I can go back to my room and go to sleep.* I couldn't pull it off, your hands came in search of me, finding me in my seasons of solitude, and then your mouth took care of the rest. The scents dazzled me, it's not easy being overwhelmed by life and death, embraced and then trying to keep your distance. Not after the decision to remain cloistered, not after all the slips and falls avoided, not after planning the wall that was supposed to save me. But save me from what, after all? From this, damn it, from this. From all this noise of the river, beautiful and mortal, that I even went in search of myself.

Liguori wasn't sleeping. He'd tried to discover weariness inside him, but it was nowhere to be found. His naked body suddenly annoyed him, he put his clothes back on.

Maybe you'll come back.

He pulled up the roller blind, which jammed at the top just to annoy him. He threw open the shutters. A black silhouette made up of the profiles of trees and plants served as a backdrop to the fickle glittering of the water. A streetlamp contained in its apron of light a church dome and a tower. The night was clear, it let itself be seen. The laughter of someone out in the street somewhere echoed from who knows where. The noise of the river was loud: a weir, a rapids, a cataract, the collapse of a dam. Blanca had foreseen it—he hadn't believed her.

He wanted to go out. It annoyed him to have to wait—he wasn't used to it. He switched on his phone, replied to a few messages, tried to concentrate. He had no desire to lose even the smallest pieces of this acceptable mood that he'd rebuilt for himself, but his thoughts kept going back to a past so recent that it was still present.

Nothing surprises me: I've said goodbye so many times, with excuses of all kinds. You, at least, just left and that was it. And you did the right thing, because waking up together can be awkward, the day dawns and things change. Before you know it the sound of the river is indistinguishable from the flushing toilet. If you come back, I'll tell you that a world of the flesh like this is something I've never known. Maybe the last few times with Marinella, when it was already all over. But no, even then it really wasn't the same. Listen closely, though, if you make me tired of the passing days again, I'll kill you and prop you up in a soccer net with a blade of grass in your mouth. A murder more, a murder less, what difference does it make? I have an exact image of your body inside my eyes, and yet I don't even know what you're like. I haven't seen you and yet I know you. At a certain point you decided to carry me along with you, and I'm as baffled as can be as to just where your mystery begins. Bites after a fast—you make love the way you eat. Part of me almost always just sits and watches, that I know: it might not be elegant, in terms of pleasure, I'm saying, but that's the way it is. That part of me laughs, too, because if you're wide awake and present you can hardly help but recognize the obscene, the unseemliness of a scream, legs excessively spread-eagled, the throes of the struggle. I can't imagine how you managed always to keep one step ahead of me, to never lose your balance even as you were losing it. How you manage to stay beautiful in the darkness. And then you were gone, but I don't think it was planned out, intentional, canny. Maybe it's as simple as you not wanting to sleep with a stranger, you don't want to, and that's that. We're not that young anymore, the way we were when we could still believe in closeness. Maybe. The fact remains that here I sat like a fool, and I'm still waiting for you and wondering whether this squandering of energy after the energy we spent so well is nothing more than a curiosity about the quirk that inhabits your head and your eyes.

Liguori closed the shutters and stretched out on the bed.

Instead, you decided to leave. What a good little girl you are.

38.

Blanca and Liguori saw each other again at breakfast—the woman expected a certain distance and she found what she'd expected. She wasn't able to swallow, the few forced bites she took pushed her nausea toward her mouth.

"Did you sleep well, Signora? Your face looks nicely rested."

"Slept very well, thank you. I see that you too have a relaxed expression this morning."

"Yes, your eyes serve you well." Liguori spoke with the smile of any ordinary distant spectator. "Tell the truth: you like pain, you like wandering around blindfolded inside the lives of others, mocking the meanness of spirit of those who fail to grasp a single aspect of your mystery. It amuses you, the malaise of distance is no contraindication. Quite the contrary."

"Now then, Detective, today we meet with Adami. We have an appointment to see him at eleven."

"Fine. Now, if you'll excuse me, I'm going to go take a walk over near where Julia Marin lived. The extracurricular details continue to interest me. See you later. If you have any difficulties getting to the police station, give me a call."

"I won't have any difficulties."

Liguori moved off. The light settled into his weary eyes and annoyed him. He likewise noticed the beauty of piazzas and streets, finding that beauty to be homogeneous.

"Where we come from, the wonderful is always undercut

by the horror nearby, the sincerity of chaos. Here, everything seems to be mature, uniformly applied; it reassures your expectations, promising more. Different forms of allure. If you want to go for subtleties, the only problem I see is this pavement, like the marble flooring in a lobby, a sort of television plaster. It must be a recent innovation."

The places where Julia Marin had lived possessed an equal share of constant beauty.

He asked around about her. Only a few were willing to talk to him, but when Liguori added that Julia Marin was the victim found in the stadium, they did their best to remember. The information he gathered yielded no interesting tidbits.

Blanca asked the housecleaner when her shift ended. Her schedule suited Blanca's need and so she asked the woman to walk her to the police station.

"Your accent isn't from around here, have you lived here long?"

"Just three years. I'm Calabrian, my son is studying at the university here."

"How do you like living here?"

"There's good things and bad things, like anywhere, like always."

The woman had no interest in talking, and when they reached the police station she refused money and left.

Captain Adami said he was quite skeptical about the likelihood of a serial killer. He didn't see the one constant that he'd seen in murders committed by serial killers: a lack of connection between the victims. Jerry and Julia in fact had actually been lovers. Liguori and Blanca studied the evidence, interviewed the captain, and told him about the events in Naples. Adami asked lots of questions about the murder of the night watchman. The detective told him that in Martusciello's opinion, it had been the work of professionals interested in leaving as few clues as possible. The captain told them that he considered organized crime to be a national catastrophe, that he wanted nothing to do with those who thought *fine, too bad for them, let them kill each other off.* This captain listened to good music.

Every so often Liguori got distracted and glanced over at Blanca.

Every so often, Blanca lacked focus because of that scent of the flesh. Adami explained that the night of Julia Marin's murder, the two guards at the Bentegodi had been drugged, the forensics team had found traces of the narcotic in a bottle of second-rate spumante, so bad, he added, that in order to forget it they would have fallen asleep even without the sleeping pills.

They worked all day. When evening came, the captain invited them to dine in the same restaurant where they'd eaten the night before.

The proprietor suggested Blanca sample the Amarone risotto.

"I had a chance to enjoy it yesterday." She turned toward Liguori. "I would rather procure a new memory."

Adami was pleasant company, and during the meal they avoided all conversation about investigations and suspects. It was only when they were saying goodnight that the captain mentioned the appointment the following day with the medical examiner.

Blanca and Liguori climbed the stairs to their floor in silence. The man stopped outside the door of the woman's room:

"You owe me a few apologies. You can make them in your room, that way you don't have to leave afterward." They spoke in the dark. They exchanged secrets and laughter and phrases without any intelligent line of defense.

Then Blanca climbed back up onto her high heels and teetered once again on the brink of the precipice.

39

I didn't do a good job of getting rid of you, I haven't completed my task. I'm no good even at slaughtering your memory. I would like to hook it up by the heels, a village hog. I wish I could hear it squeal.

I wish I could overturn the bowl set to capture the liquids that spilt from the dying animal.

I'd like to fall asleep right in front of the severed jugular.

Instead the memories survive and here they are, stomping on every part of me, curse them.

"Does your neck hurt?" I asked you after the two men had left and we were alone in the dense darkness that you had desired. As usual.

"Cuts are always a serious matter, but what could you know about it, since you spend all your time in a closed cabinet," you told me. "Blades, even if they don't plunge deep into the flesh, remain. Under the throat. Like a long goodbye." I couldn't see a thing, but I could smell the stench of your fear.

There in the dark you grabbed me.

"Now get down there and do what you have to do."

"At your orders, sir."

Of course I liked it. I liked it. And it destroyed me.

And it made me become another person. Terrible. Indecent. A liar. Of course, I'm not such an idiot that I don't know I'm others as well as myself, just like everyone is, probably. Even before you, I mean. The other me's were hanging on hooks in the *walnut-wood armoire: lovely little outfits, nicely ironed, sweet smelling. Every so often I'd take down one that had caught my fancy. The threat began when I chose, when you started choosing the same one every time, always the same one, always the same one.*

I lost all the rest while you took everything. And you talked. You demanded. And you sliced open.

And I loved with a crystalline rage your stench of fear.

At the end you said to me:
"What a good little boy you are."
"I'm your property, sir." You opened the window to the light and went on not seeing me.

40.

"You've started to go out on weekends again, Martusciello. That's good."

"Well? If there's one thing that rattles my nervous system it's this good and bad you know so much about."

Santina was cleaning up in the kitchen, the captain was answering her from the dining room, channel surfing with the volume turned down low. The woman lowered her own volume and went on talking, sure that her husband would get up from the sofa and move into the hallway to hear better, unseen.

"You have this thing about bodily illnesses being evidence of your virility leaving you. You can't accept the idea that it might be an imperfection in just a part of you, no, sir: you feel as if you're a machine, a high performance car, and even the smallest cog or gear has to be made of gold, absolutely impervious to wear and tear. Otherwise the engine is going to stop working. Otherwise the litany of the passing years is going to start up: so few are left, so many have gone by, I just can't do it anymore, and so on and so forth. And what the hell! You've always been healthy, what's the big deal, it's just a minor operation for . . . and after all the problem was solved in a week. You let your weariness drag on for two months. Far too long. So I'm just happy to see you back at work, going out, doing what you need to do. Coming and going is your daily bread, you seemed like a kid without toys. That's what."

Santina took her sweet time understanding. If something

happened that didn't entirely convince her, first she sank into a state of immobility, then she reluctantly took step after step toward the point of pain. In the end, she understood. And once she understood, she turned hard, in part because of all the wasted time. Perhaps a massive intelligence takes days to get started. Then the woman gave birth to her answer, a wrinkled tortoise. She licked up the placenta and never gave it another thought.

At that point, she became brisk and dismissive, eager to regain time. Martusciello didn't answer, to deny his wife the satisfaction of knowing he was interested in her words.

The sound of the telephone came as a benediction.

"Captain, this is Funicella Corta."

"Where are you?"

"I am where I am and don't bother writing down the number, it won't do you any good anyway. In five minutes I'm going to throw away the SIM card I just bought. I'm in a world of trouble, but that's not why I'm calling you, Captain. I don't have anything to do with the betting sheets of the illegal gambling rings and the people they're arresting. I'm going to take myself out of circulation for a while, far from everybody else, and by the time I get back it's all going to be cleared up."

"I'm delighted to hear you have such faith in the criminal justice system."

"Of course I do! I know that you came by the house and that my sister played emissary. A tiny heart threw out her hands without permission; the other parts of the organism flew into a rage, look out. Around here, the independent masters can't decide which steps to take on their own; the brain has to tell them where to go. Otherwise, the machine shuts down because of an unwanted malfunction."

"What is this, have you been talking to Santina?"

"What?"

"No, nothing, I was just thinking."

"Captain, I only have one thing to tell you: I had nothing to do with it. Let's take Malanò's answer, it's best for everyone."

"Funice', this does me no good. And even if it did, it wouldn't even occur to me in the slightest to call it something that it's not. Are we clear on this? By all means, tell Sconciglio too."

"As you like, I had a debt and now I've paid it off. Do as you see best. *Buona sera.*" Funicella Corta cut off the call, pulled the SIM card out of his phone, and tossed it into the waves off Marseilles.

Martusciello caught up with Santina in the bathroom; she'd just finished cleaning up the kitchen and now she was about to smear her hands with lotion in a gesture that she repeated every night.

She set down the container and embraced her husband, who smiled at her.

"I'm just intolerable when I'm being a wife."

"You're lovely, Santina. In your presence, I turn into an imbecile and I enjoy it all the same."

"I'm . . . "

Martusciello stopped her from talking with one hand, and then the prohibition turned into a caress.

41

Rosina Mastriani had developed the habit of not spending her day in Pianura. Every morning she got dressed and went into the quarters of town where her husband trafficked. She wanted to see, one by one, all his rotten apples. Rosina Mastriani needed convincing arguments. She was no innocent, but she wanted to redeem with her ruins the shortcomings of others.

Her husband told her that he knew she had murdered her boyfriend. What the children had lost was a mother with her picture on the front pages of all the newspapers and luckily what he had lost was an ugly cow.

By revisiting the well known streets, Rosina managed to overcome the stunned daze of her first return.

Almost every day, she tried to walk past his apartment building, no longer his. She'd been going to look at it for as long as she could remember. The old building had a narrow side that gave the structure a *v* shape: in the girl's imagination, under her short cropped hair, it was the throne of the sun. The opening toward the exterior of the outside walls formed wings, jammed into the earth that belonged to him.

I suffocated the violence, enormous and cast iron, I managed the rage within a narrow body. I should have expected that Vialdi would understand immediately. Her husband amused the singer. He took him into his business dealings, which Rosina hadn't understood all that clearly. She knew only that there was money and there were possessions. An enormous quantity of possessions: televisions, blenders, stoves, clothing, toys, motorcycles, jewelry.

For Vialdi, his friendship with Rosina's husband meant a chance to go back to the places he'd started out from, and when he came back he wanted to be dressed in his best gala wear. It was hardly necessary, his fame had taken him for strolls in far more magnificent venues, but he want to be acknowledged as king in those places where he had once been nothing more than the son of Concetta Mangiavento, aka Sette Carceri.

At first, Vialdi just looked at her and nothing more. By the time he started talking to her secretly, his eyes had already told the whole story. A fever grew inside Rosina, whispering incessantly *you of all people, you of all people.*

Her heart was stirring, even though she had no longer had any idea of how to love, even that tiniest bit that could distract her from her troubles.

She felt pretty. The color that she'd once had in the mornings as she set off for school, on her way to meet progress, returned to her face.

The Sanità district shed its destiny and became the beautiful center of every city in the world. That was where this unexpected story of the heart was taking place.

Love changed her eyes.

She began only to see lovely streets, narrow and cheerful. She drew close to the people who had wedded the traditional cult of the remains of the Fontanelle Ossuary with the desire for the new. She got to know the ordinary people who prepared meals for the homeless, ordinary just like her. She went to pay a call on a priest who had organized a magnificent revolution, with the local kids in tow, and he explained to her the history of art, with warm words of the kind that she'd long ago forgotten.

The story of the heart had infected all the places of her

birth: now Rosina could not recognize anything that wasn't beautiful.

Her children had the benefit of a brand-new mother, just learning to love. Then came Vialdi's transformation, his loss of interest, the disappointment that brought her thudding back to earth. Her eyes closed. When they opened again, Rosina realized that she'd also lost her obedience, her children, and her home. All that remained to her were the cuts on her arms.

Her affair with the singer went on until it withered and died. During one of their last encounters, the chemical that he'd taken before the appointment led Vialdi to confide in Rosina about her husband. If he'd been straight, he'd never have done it.

"He helps out the bosses of certain gambling rings. He's a two-bit crook, don't be fooled, he makes his little bit of cash and invests it in small-time loan-sharking, they pay him in trinkets and knickknacks. These days the local craftsmen have all been outsourced, they're part of a larger business cycle. He just picks up the crumbs left over from the network." At the time, the information hadn't been of any interest to her: it was just a length of rope that was already too taut leading toward the end of her love affair.

Then knowing became important.

Persisting in her visits to the Sanità neighborhood, Rosina finally hit pay dirt. Vialdi had told the truth, at least when he told her what he did about her husband's business activities: he had something like a subcontract on collecting gambling debts, shaking down shopkeepers, money from bets of all kinds that just didn't seem to want to come to papa. In the comings and goings of relatively small sums, he had a license to subtract a 5 percent commission. Frequently retailers paid off what they owed in kind, and therefore: televisions, blenders, stoves, clothing, toys, motorcycles, jewelry. Her husband invested the cash by loaning out small sums at exorbitant rates.

The last service announcement, as unwelcome as all the

others, took her to Santa Lucia. The address had been given to her by a seamstress in the Sanità neighborhood. But Rosina decided, as she looked out over the waves, that what she knew already was enough, and so she went to the Borgo Marinari.

The morning's beauty, the bridge to cross on foot to fetch up beneath the magnificence of Castel dell'Ovo, the boats, the sea—it all restored a bit of her strength.

She drank in the ancient beauty of the gold that, before experiencing the love of the sun, had been nothing but stone. A single solitary cloud was casting its shadow on a single solitary tower, darkness too wanted to get a taste of the glittering yellow. She felt hungry. She greeted the need in her saliva.

"Dear singer of mine, though mine you never were, if you've learned how to die, maybe my husband can learn the same lesson. I'd be glad to offer him a little tutoring. Then I could follow him down." She went in search of her spouse and sure enough she found him.

She poured over his head the whole bucket of things she'd discovered, covered his feet with the whole barrel of bad apples. He seized her by the neck and told her how sorry he was, but now she had become the villain of the story. That she should have thought carefully before becoming a vigilante out for justice. When she was still a saintly, weary mother, when someone might still have listened to a thing she said.

On her way back home, Rosina passed the castle again, and the desire to go to some discarded king and ask for help surged within her. The temptation inebriated her, but in her drunkenness she realized that she lacked the strength for a new term of imprisonment.

All the same, she needed to find a place to hide, she wouldn't be able to make it on her own. Or else she needed to get her hands on a gun.

42.

Marialuigia Moreno drew marks in the dust with her fingernail. She hadn't used the piano again since. She felt a twinge of regret for having neglected it. She grabbed her wrist in the fist of her other hand and ran her forearm over the fall covering the keyboard.

She opened it.

Without sitting down, she tried out the keys. They responded well, the piano was still in tune. She pulled up the bench, felt for the pedals with her feet, and started to play.

She picked the chords she loved least, the ones that made up the song that had bought Vialdi his double-decker penthouse. She played a blues arrangement of the song, the music and the intentional off-key notes violated the silence of the melancholy become sound.

Every twelve beats, she let the words drop from her mouth, in a sung sigh, *Tu sei tu*. Only those words, no more. The other words were all ugly, they'd have fogged the black and white of the keys, as well as the sentiment that was driving her voice.

She tried to stop but she couldn't do it.

She sat there keeping company with her memories for a period of time she was unable to reckon with any accuracy, then she tore herself away from the piano and went off once again to break the seals on an apartment that did not belong to her.

Captain Malanò was enjoying the sound of the waves from

his studio apartment with its galley kitchen. Stretched out on his couch, he listed the fruit of his imminent happiness.

He was going to have, he was going to be able to, he was going to say, he was going to defeat, he was going to exult in triumph.

The prophecy of all things good had been undermined, if only slightly, by his memory of the phone call with Adami: after meeting with Liguori and Occhiuzzi he'd felt obliged to tell him what he thought about the serial killer. Adami told him that he'd already laid out the facts that didn't convince him to Occhiuzzi and Liguori.

"Oh, that's no big thing," Malanò told himself, deeply hooked, "a serial killer could certainly fixate on a family, with people who have something to do with the same line of work, or who knows what all else. What do I care about what does or doesn't happen in statistical terms? Who gives a damn about statistics! Even the murder of the drunk night watchman might very well be connected to something entirely different. This Adami is such a nitpicker. He thinks everything's neat and settled. Easy to say! I'm feeling my way here, looking for logic where there might not even be any. And that's that."

Martusciello heard the breathing of his wife, fast asleep by his side. He didn't want to awaken her, but his thoughts refused to leave him alone in sleep, and his feet followed his thoughts in their restlessness, in spite of him.

I'd like to know what relationship there is in my body between noggin and my dogs! he thought to himself. What a bad habit I have: I can't seem to think clearly if my feet aren't moving.

The captain gave in to the restlessness of his feet. He got out of bed, groped for his clothing in the dark, got dressed and spruced up in the bathroom, and a short while later was out in the street.

He stopped a taxi and asked to be taken to a gambling hall near the stadium.

"I hear you, friend. I always come to this part of town to do my betting, too. The betting sheet has an entirely different kind of poetry, in the shadow of the San Paolo stadium. If you want a sure thing I suggest that you go play Series B at Zivi's. Tell them that I sent you. My taxi number is Modena 19."

"Now that I have a recommendation I feel more confident."

"I'm just telling you things that anyone could tell you: it's just because Zivi's is open round the clock, and after all, I wouldn't want you to have come all this way for nothing, right?"

The streets around the stadium were empty and the neon streetlights made them look uglier than they were. The captain kept walking until he was able to calm down feet and head. He saw his theories collapse, like oil on water. They took unexpected shapes, and were in any case insubstantial, changeable.

The slight uphill climbs toward the stadium made his thoughts move laboriously. For some time now, the captain had lost the benefit of his confidence in the facts. A good mood might change his outlook on decline and turn it into a fun slide, but that didn't happen often, and certainly never when he was sensing the presence of some preordained confusion.

While Liguori and Blanca were on their way back from Verona she had called him from the highway to tell him how it had gone. She also told him about the conversation with Adami.

His northern colleague's misgivings weren't far from his own. Martusciello could smell a nicely crafted farce, put together with an abundance of resources. He'd recognized a beautifully prepared banqueting table, even before he accepted a case he didn't really want: the presence of just one night watchman on the night of the murder, found murdered, note the coincidence, with an unorthodox caliber; the corpses of the Singing Maestro and Julia Marin both tricked out in a manner designed to scream scandal, passion, and insanity; Vialdi's personality and fame and sins spotlighted in every statement, practically with the same identical words. Every element seemed to have been buffed and polished and put right in its place. Too shiny, too perfect.

"Maybe it's because the village donkeys have no time to waste," thought Martusciello. "They don't look only at the hand that makes the rabbit pop into view, and if someone forces them with the right lights, they'll get up on all fours, after all they have something to do with their heads, trot around, and place themselves behind the stage. And they take a stab."

After coming to an acceptable conclusion, which as we need hardly point out, was radically different from the one that Malanò was trying so hard to find, he walked into the betting parlor.

He spoke to a man who had the air of an habitué.

"Vialdi told me to come, I'm looking for the lawyer."

"Vialdi's dead and the lawyer wouldn't be here at this time of night."

The man lifted his shoulders into a shrug and he was gone before they dropped back down.

43.

The drive home from Verona had been slow. On the highway, Liguori had kept the car in the right lane and motored along at a moderate speed.

"And this time, I get to choose the soundtrack: Sarah Vaughan. With all due respect to Mozart. Okay with you?"

"Sure, but lower the volume."

"But she's whispering."

"Not to my ears."

Blanca decided that he actually had spoken softly the night before, when he asked her: *Let me see you. Just for a few seconds. For a moment.*

She needed to tidy up that confusion, she needed to reestablish a provisional *before* that she could never regain.

"Liguori, nobody'd better find out about this at the office. Or anywhere else."

"You're forgetting that I'm a knight and a gentleman. I may lack a horse, but with me chivalry isn't dead, as our boss likes to say." The detective was mortified, a tad, by the relief her request had brought him.

"Well, what do you think, was the trip useful?" asked Blanca.

"Extremely."

"In terms of work, I mean."

"I'll lie to Martusciello, but the trip to Verona didn't do us a bit of good, and I knew it wouldn't before we left. The place that most of my questions lead to isn't Verona, but Naples. Why can't we find the recording of Vialdi's last show? I've looked for it everywhere. It hasn't done any good. And yet the singer wanted to use the recording for a live album."

"Live."

"Live, yeah. How could he have known that he was going to be dead in just a few hours?"

Not even Blanca knew. Liguori thought of her "yes": she'd covered her face with her hands and had given him a moment in which to indulge in the pleasure of watching her. He couldn't know that he'd lit a central beam of light, powerful and pitiless, and had laid eyes everywhere. Everyone has their own way of dealing with confusion.

Despite the harshness of the spotlight, a bit of harmony still survived, the motionless white body preserved shreds of grace, even after the haste and sweat of the gestures.

"*...but you're not getting it from me and no one needs to say you're on again.*" Blanca out of tune singing Sarah Vaughan. "Have you been to the Auditorium too?"

"Yep, and it's not in the archives. They told me that the recording technicians weren't staff. Whether they were outside professionals or staff, I can't understand why there isn't the slightest trace of the concert."

"Maybe it wasn't much to write home about."

"You've been spending too much time with Martusciello."

"Maybe they were planning other shows and the technicians, who might not have been on staff, decided for some reason to postpone the recording to another night. What do I know, too much applause, too much external noise, some malfunction."

"I hadn't thought of that, it might be. But why wouldn't they have told me?"

"Maybe it strikes them as unimportant. When Vialdi died, a lot of people lost their jobs, and now they have other things to worry about. Maybe there are people who think of work as something more than a place to work on puzzles."

"Yep, you've been spending too much time with Martusciello."

"Now I'll call him, so I can tell him all about Verona and the time we wasted."

44

Rosina Mastriani wasn't expecting an unannounced visit from a police detective and she had no intention of letting him in.

She looked at her messy apartment and her arms, riddled with cuts.

"I don't have to let you in."

She was laboriously won over by Liguori's insistence; he pretended to take no notice of the tangled welter of drinking glasses, clothing, newspapers, and dirty dishes.

Rosina Mastriani turned off the television set and, with her back to him, covered her arms as best she could with her three-quarter-length sleeves.

"You're hurt."

"I was plowing the playground. What do you want? Let's get this out of the way, I have things to do."

"I want to know if you attended Vialdi's last concert."

"No. *Arrivederci.*"

Liguori shoved aside a pile of clothes and got comfortable on the filthy couch. "I'm not trying to scare you, but you're not in a very comfortable position."

Rosina Mastriani laughed. "Neither are you, the springs on that couch are broken. I don't even know what a comfortable position means. I've never known and it's no clearer to me now. You see, my dear handsome detective, prison doesn't really look all that bad. I'm about to lose the apartment. I'm unemployed and lately I've had to add Person of Interest in a Murder

Investigation to my CV, and that doesn't help much in an already challenging job market. The press has had a lot of fun at my expense."

"I could help you."

Rosina Mastriani laughed harder this time:

"The last time somebody said that to me I wound up with a car I couldn't afford and I lost what little I had to my name."

"What car?"

"This one," the woman pointed to a picture. "I put it up for sale, but no one wants it."

"I'll buy it from you."

"And what do you want in exchange?"

"Nothing." The woman walked Liguori to the door:

"Do you really want to buy the car?"

"Yes, tomorrow I'll bring you a down payment." Without even knowing why, Rosina Mastriani decided that the detective really was going to.

Mara Scacchi didn't look up and automatically repeated her query—*prego?*—to the man standing at the counter.

"I'm Detective Liguori, we met at the Pozzuoli police station, about the Vialdi case."

"I have nothing to add to what I've already told you."

Liguori picked up a box of analgesics from a display case next to the cash register.

"Are these good for headaches?"

"Yes, that'll be seven euros fifty."

"Fine. So we'll see you tomorrow at the police station. And do me a favor, don't come in before eleven. You understand, with these migraines . . . "

The pharmacist lifted the hinged section of the counter top and invited the detective to follow her back to a private area, crowded with shelves and drawers. Her father took her place serving the public, after giving her a hard stare.

"Spare me the trip. *Whodunit? The Pharmacist?* is already a book title I'm sick and tired of reading."

"Did you go see Jerry Vialdi's last concert at the Auditorium?"

"Yes, I went. I didn't want to deny myself a healthy helping of musical gall. Vialdi used to invite all his women. He liked to scatter music and glances."

"Did you notice anything you'd like to tell me about?"

"Nothing special: if you've seen one of the Maestro's concerts, you've seen them all. You know, it almost scared me the way he could repeat himself, exactly the same every time. The only thing that would change was the beginning. He'd sing two or three numbers from his latest CD, then the rest never varied. You could even predict the pauses, they always arrived at the exact same moment. Stuff that would make anybody want to kill him."

"We can't seem to track down the recording."

"Don't ask me about it."

"Would you help me find it?"

"Why should I?"

"Because if you weren't the one who mixed up the stuff that killed him, it might be nice to have your name cleared of murder."

"You're not going to find anything in the recording, don't get your hopes up. And even if there was something inopportune, Vialdi's staff would already have taken care of any surprises. They're good, you know, and if there's one thing they hate it's approximation." The pharmacist, her father, came toward the shelves and Mara Scacchi held out her hand to Liguori to get rid of him with a handshake.

The detective noticed her dilated pupils.

Liguori parked outside Nini's friend's house and sat in the car waiting for his doubts to disperse.

Blanca had told him about Tita's fear for her mother, but she'd told him in the dark, out of a nagging personal worry.

She'd told him about her visit, the apartment and the woman's tension. She'd also asked him to keep that information to himself.

The detective's hesitation lasted the duration of three songs by Nina Simone, then it was replaced by his usual impatience to take care of things. He knew very well what the urge to rummage through things, look for missing pieces was all about. Ever since he'd chosen his job, work that Martusciello considered an aristocratic luxury, he was all too familiar with the desire to conquer his own disorder, and life in general.

He got out of the car and headed toward the apartment building where Tita's mother lived, already imagining Blanca's reaction when she found out about it. So he came up with a remedy.

"Signora Datri? *Buon giorno*, I'm Deputy Giuseppe Càrita from the Pozzuoli police station. Sergeant Blanca Occhiuzzi asked me to drop by." The woman met Liguori on the landing. Her housedress was flapping open and she didn't bother to button it, her arms were dangling at her sides and her eyes looked helpless.

"I'm not feeling well, is this going to take very long?"

"Of course, my apologies. I'd just like to know if by any chance you attended Jerry Vialdi's last concert at the Auditorium."

The woman assumed an enchanted expression, she didn't even feel the need to nod. For Maria Datri it was unthinkable that she could have missed any chance to chase after the destiny that was custom stitched to suit her.

Liguori decided he'd made an unproductive trip that Blanca wouldn't have appreciated: the woman wasn't sound of mind.

"Do you know anything that might be useful to our investigation?"

"I don't know anything anymore."

The detective regretted having this urge of his to rummage through weak disorders, even in those who, perhaps because of those very disorders, might have killed.

45.

Martusciello got a tighter grip on the handrail. A jerk of the subway train had caused him to stumble over the suitcase of a traveler who had boarded with him at the central train station, while he was asking for information about the Campi Flegrei stop.

A man in a threadbare jacket felt obliged not only to count the stops between there and Campi Flegrei, but also to give a tourist, in a broken mix of languages, a rundown on the history and geography of the place, both seismic in nature.

"Flègo: to fire. To set the fire, to burn, to catch fire. Phlegraean Fields is a big crater, kilometers and kilometers across, I don't recall now, but maybe twenty, to compare Vesuvio, do you know Vesuvio? it's a child dragon, *un drago creaturo*, spit only a little fire. *Ci sono nato.* I was born here, qua, *settantotto anni fa*, almost eighty year. *Tanto tiempo.* Do you know tanto tiempo? The station where you have to get out is so beautiful, *bella assai*. Once real trains came here too, which was right, *mi pareva pure giusto*, because the station of Mergellina, the trains went there, and the station of Campi Flegrei is much more expressive—*espressivo*—than the central station, even if now they have put in it the stores that you can find anyplace, *da tutte le parti. Chi è nato qua*, who was born here, knows that they are always on top of a train with the binary, the . . . the . . . the *tracks* of fire. They know, there's no need for the mamma to explain. Mother knows."

The tourist didn't understand a word of it, but he was appreciative of the effort and the smile from under the hat tipped in farewell, before getting out at the Campi Flegrei stop.

Martusciello didn't follow him toward the exit. Instead he went over to where a side track terminated and smoked a cigarette in the company of a line of abandoned subway cars.

The call was an interruption. The phone flashed its useless alerts.

"Funicella, all these mysteries knock me off balance. If you want to talk, just talk and be done with it. And try to call me with a SIM card my phone recognizes, because this 'unknown caller' is starting to ruin my health."

A short while later he walked into the gambling parlor. He climbed up onto an uncomfortable stool facing screens with a blend of soccer players and racehorses.

He had the whole morning to wait for the lawyer.

Experts, commentators, kids, opinion-mongers, dilettantes, ordinary-looking women with grocery bags waiting in corners alongside bookies, white slaves, clerks, moneyless spectators, and retirees: all of them launching into solo performances like so many seers with an array of preconceived certainties. They warded off bad luck with improvised weapons, speaking without saying a word to anyone else.

The lawyer came over and placed one foot on the crossbar of the uncomfortable stool.

He stared at the captain. Martusciello returned his insistent stare: he ran his eyes over the grey suit, a little too tight around waist and legs, the tieless shirt, the week's growth of whiskers that somehow didn't manage to add years to the facial features, regular and marked by recent neglect. He considered the skinny face and body, the brisk, unselfconscious movements that would have been beyond him even when he was the same age as this young man.

The lawyer went on staring at him.

"I'm Luigi D'Amore. Were you looking for me, Captain?"

"How would you know?"

"In gambling parlors, word gets around, it's the way they work." He put on a smile, and the smile refused to go away.

"Does the way they work also involve providing controlled substances to a singer recently found dead and tangled in the net of a soccer goalpost?"

The lawyer started delivering a sermon against addiction. The lesson he was laying out for Martusciello followed a sensible structure. The lawyer's perennial smile only became sunnier with terms like pathological condition, loss of control, rootlessness, and personal weakness.

The captain interrupted the lecture but couldn't do anything about the smile.

"Were you taking care of Vialdi's interests?"

"In part, I'm a point of reference for the people who run the parlors, I only met Vialdi because he liked to bet regularly. That's all."

"Large sums?"

"It depends, to someone like him who got paid thousand of euros just to take a breath, they might not have been big sums. To me they were."

"You are a paragon of moral rectitude, Counselor."

"Necessarily. I attended law school on the earnings of my mother, who worked all her life as a waitress."

"Vialdi wasn't exactly born into the lap of luxury either, I believe."

"Jerry Vialdi was already a rich man when I was still shoplifting university textbooks."

"Ah, you see, you're capable of the occasional misdemeanor yourself. I'm glad to hear it. I'm afraid of people who say they've never cracked an egg."

"Sure, I've cracked a few in my time, but we're on the same

side, Captain." The smile faded on the drawn features, but it brightened almost immediately.

"I'm glad to hear you know what side I'm on, most of the time I don't even know myself."

"I'm at your complete disposal, Captain." He handed Martusciello a business card, but the captain still wasn't done.

"How did you know I was going to drop by here?"

"Don't underestimate yourself, your tenacity is well known, at least in the circles where you move. In any case, even if you hadn't come looking for me where you found me, I'd have come to see you."

Counselor Luigi D'Amore's sunny helpfulness landed on Martusciello's aching feet, and in his irritation he tried another shot in the dark.

"You're also a lawyer for the Sconciglio family, aren't you?"

"Well, not for the whole Sconciglio family. I'm Giovanni's lawyer: he operates legally licensed gambling parlors just about everywhere."

"Ah, so you're the lawyer for Don Giovanni. Then I was right, it's more or less like representing the legal interests of the whole family."

"I don't follow you."

"That can happen, sometimes there are a lot of different roads that lead to the same destination. So what do you have in mind when you say 'just about everywhere'?"

"Campania, Lazio, Lombardy . . . "

"Veneto . . . "

"Sure, Veneto too, I think."

The lawyer's smile remained in place while his hand reached around for the handle of his briefcase.

46

Rosina Mastriani tidied up her apartment, got dressed and ready, and sat down to wait for the detective and his money.

She opened the windows and was astonished at the fresh lightness of the breeze, so different from the air that so often oppressed Pianura. The leafy breeze from the trees in the adjoining Park of the Astroni had begun to blow on a day that Rosina Mastriani would not soon forget.

She found the courage to phone home and ask about the children. Her husband told her that she no longer had the right.

"Let me see them."

The woman recited a litany of her faults and misdeeds, she talked and talked until the cuts that she inflicted on herself on a daily basis began forming new flesh.

"I don't believe that they don't want me anymore." Her husband laughed and hung up the phone.

Rosina Mastriani relived her capacity to always display the worst parts of herself, to take punches in silence to keep from waking the children, the daily violence of her husband's return home, unwilling to answer her prayers never to see him again, never never again. She revived in her memory her broken prayers, the nauseating lack of courage to do anything, the spare change left on the night table, mortifying her, worse than being kicked, and the illusion that in Jerry Vialdi she'd found a little bit of heaven.

I can't say a thing to you. The whore that left home is me. And I can't shout the curses that fill my mind: even the children were yours, as well as the rest of the pain and grief, and in my joy I didn't even want them anymore. It's all disgusting, I know, but you're part of it just as much as I am.

Liguori noticed the change in the woman, even more unmistakable than the new face that the apartment had put on. He handed her the down payment on her car and confirmed that before the week was up he'd be done with the change in title.

Rosa Mastriani was wearing a short-sleeved shirt, her arms showing scars and fresh cuts. By now she'd made it clear to herself: she wouldn't be able to make it on her own, she might as well display all the fear she was capable of.

"By law, am I allowed to see my children?"

"Have you already completed the divorce process? Have you been denied parental custody and visiting rights?"

"I'm not legally divorced. I simply left."

"I can introduce you to some people who can help you. But now why don't you flip the picture and tell me exactly who Jerry Vialdi really was and where the hell I can find the recording of the concert."

As she was answering, Rosina Mastriani considered how her words were venturing into places and thoughts that before she opened her mouth she hadn't thought she knew. The woman told him about a fragile man, who went searching for courage in the applause, in the desire to please no matter the cost; even the chemicals he ingested were a way to keep from disobeying that role.

The singer's arrogant bullying was different from her husband's: the way he inflicted it was by denying her his presence, triggering the malaise of need. He let her chase after him. And she'd been only too glad to do the chasing. The need she'd given in to was her third mistake as a mother.

Liguori watched Rosina Mastriani's facial features change as she went on talking. They put on or shed years. The red of her hair and her freckles took part in the transformation.

The information about the possibility of looking for the recording prompted a flat conclusion:

"Ask his personal servant, ask Gatta Mignon. And don't believe her for an instant when she starts meowing, she has a cast-iron head."

When Liguori left, the woman thanked him in her mind for having delved honestly into all those memories that had once been so blurry to her eyes, thanked him as many times as was necessary, and finally managed to break into tears after an endless lifetime that had been condensed into three years.

Then she slowly dialed her home phone number. He husband didn't speak a word, but Rosa Mastriani could hear him breathing:

"I'm going to come get them. If they still want me."

47

Martusciello's summertime defeat and the frantic oppression that had been growing ever since that initial moment of disgust in the sheet metal shack all vanished in a rediscovered determination to defeat the lawyer's smile.

The captain decided that he wanted to find a way to unsettle Nino Sparaco, recently hauled in as part of the investigation into illegal betting and gambling rings. Despite the hours-long deposition, Sparaco was careful not to let the slightest hint of a piece of useful information escape his lips, he just drank water and sweated the whole time. He had a fear in him that made him careful.

And so the captain turned to Lieutenant Guidi of the Guardia di Finanza, the financial police, who had arrested Sparaco in the first place. Guidi was a man he had worked with a number of other times. The lieutenant told Martusciello that they were looking into the well tested cliché of money laundering and business operations linked to the illegal betting rings, the account books that were adjusted to reflect the bets in question.

"Some defective mechanism must have slipped into standard operating procedure, but no one's talking, we can't find anything better, and the investigation is at a standstill. We're arranging new wiretaps and arrests, but I think we've got a long wait ahead of us."

"Does Luigi D'Amore, Esquire, have anything to do with this?"

"He always seems to get off scot-free, but we're looking into his case too." The captain decided to show his hand, but he asked his colleague to keep it quiet:

"Luigi D'Amore was the lawyer of Jerry Vialdi, the Singing Maestro found dead in the San Paolo Stadium."

"Malanò is in charge of that case, if I'm not mistaken. Look out for Malanò. Now, I'd be the last person to deny that the motorcycle-riding police captain is an ethical person: when he plants his claw in your eye he takes great care to hit dead center in your pupil, that way the mark is less obvious and everyone continues to think he's such a nice guy. In a number of ways, he resembles Counselor D'Amore. I can tell you that Vialdi was a heavy better, and that recently he'd even been winning. He alternated legal and illegal betting."

"So why didn't you tell the motorcycle-riding police captain about it?"

"Maybe because he wasn't especially interested in knowing about it, in fact, quite the contrary."

"Yes, I can believe that. Malanò hates anyone who tries to take away his landscape painting signed by the serial killer."

"In that case, we never met and we never talked. Though in a while we may have an opportunity to meet formally: I'm going to need Occhiuzzi's help on a few wiretaps. Is it true that Liguori is cozying up to Malanò past the point of what's acceptable?"

"You think?"

"I hear."

48

B lanca had a sweater with two pockets, one for her old phone, and one for the new phone, specially designed for the partially blind. They'd been offering her that phone since it was an experimental prototype, but she'd always refused it. She'd decided to get one when she got back from Verona, because for private reasons she couldn't have her messages read to her.

"They need to work on the privacy function, though," she'd said to Nini, who was showing her the vocal translation of the phone's functions.

"Why don't you just turn down the sound, so no one can hear it but you?"

Still, Blanca had taken care not to give Liguori her new phone number: if the old one had been good enough until now, it could go on being so.

She responded to the faint buzz of the old cell phone. When it squirmed in her pocket, the vein in her neck had throbbed in response. By now, no one used the old number but the detective.

"Check Marialuigia Moreno's address and come downstairs."

Blanca checked, then lingered with Carità long enough to make sure she wasn't prompt.

Liguori was waiting for her out front, and escorted her to the car.

"The address?"

"Same as Vialdi's." Blanca noticed that the detective's tone of voice, as he reported to her on his conversation with Rosina Mastriani, was distant. And it remained equally distant when he told her that he'd come up empty-handed in his search for the recording of the concert.

"It was Mastriani who recommended I talk to Gatta Mignon to find out what had become of it."

"Lately, you seem to enjoy wasting time. If she has the recording, or if she knows where it is and won't give it to us, I don't see why she should change her mind now."

"That's why we we're going to see her together, and you can figure out the things that aren't clear."

Lately, you seem to enjoy wasting time was Blanca's reference to Verona, but the man seemed to have missed it.

They pulled up outside of Vialdi's apartment building together, but Liguori couldn't find the name he was looking for.

"Nothing. Are you sure she lives here?"

"Yes, I checked. Martusciello told me that the surname Moreno was listed. What's the panel of buzzers look like?"

"How do I know what it looks like? It looks like a normal panel of door buzzers, with names."

"Are the names inserted into holders, superimposed, glued on, is there a plastic cover, is there a glass front, is the panel steel or some other material, is it screwed on?"

"The buzzer panel is made of brass and is meant to look classical, but it's just ugly. Each buzzer has the name set in a Plexiglas holder screwed in with . . . wait a minute, these screws are slightly raised compared with the others."

"Fine, go ahead and ring."

The lovely voice of Marialuigia Moreno answered. Blanca waved both hands in the air to indicate more, longer. She wanted to go on listening to her. Liguori didn't understand the reason behind that gesture, but before asking which staircase and floor, he engaged her in a superfluous conversation: it would have been protracted in any case because the woman had no intention of letting them come up.

Blanca broke in:

"We've just been over to Vialdi's apartment, the seals have been broken again. We're coming up."

While they were on the stairs, Liguori complained that Martusciello hadn't been keeping him informed of every detail in the case, such as the breaking of the seals, in contrast with what he must be doing with Blanca. Blanca replied that the captain's ways of working sometimes didn't allow for participation. "Lately, you speak in revealed truths, and also lately, you seem to like wasting time."

Blanca smiled without letting the smile appear on her lips.

Marialuigia Moreno ushered the two of them into an apartment filled with cardboard boxes, suitcases, and furniture packed for shipment. Only the piano was free of paper, cardboard, and tape. On the lid sat a wilted pot of daisies.

She apologized for her unwillingness to receive them. It's just that she was getting ready to move. She explained that this was her way of defeating all the endings that had befallen her lately: the death of her employer had dictated a conclusion to a profound emotional partnership and also to her source of employment.

Liguori interrupted Marialuigia Moreno with a particularly well crafted half-smile.

"Were you in charge of recording the concerts?"

"I often helped on postproduction work to improve the sound quality." Blanca walked over the piano and ran her fingers over the edge of the keyboard in a caress. Liguori went on with his distracted peppering of questions.

"And of course, you attended all of Vialdi's concerts?"

"Yes, all of them. That was my job."

"Then you must have the recording of his last concert?"

Marialuigia Moreno arched her back.

Liguori noticed just how much Gatta Mignon really did resemble the scrawniest, and therefore the most cunning, cat in the litter.

"I looked for it myself, unsuccessfully, but I wasn't all that surprised. I knew that they'd been planning to produce a live album, Vialdi's last concert was in fact the first one of his new tour. We were going to stay three nights in Naples, at the RAI Auditorium, then we'd travel on to various Italian regions, and after that, we'd go abroad. The first concert is never ripe, even the musical arrangements need to be broken in. Maybe the sound technician thought the recording was unsatisfactory, or maybe there'd been a malfunction of some kind. During the rehearsals, for example, the technician had filtered out all ambient sound, an amateur's mistake."

"You were in charge of recording even during the rehearsals," Blanca noted.

"Recording and archiving the recording are two different things," Marialuigia Moreno pointed out, in a voice that verged on the cheery. "That's all."

"That's *almost* all." Blanca didn't like to let other people draw her conclusions for her. "Captain Martusciello told us about a certain lawyer . . . "

Moreno noticed Blanca's limited sight, the woman stretched out her hands a bit too obviously when she moved from one place to another.

"Look out for the stool legs. They're sticking out. I don't know if he's *certain* or anything else, but I imagine you're talking about Counselor Luigi D'Amore, Vialdi's lawyer. But D'Amore's bar membership is available to anyone who asks."

Liguori laughed in a way that froze Blanca's blood and made it clear to her just how little she really knew the man.

"Funny," said the detective. "I'm not kidding, I really do appreciate it when someone uses another person's words in retaliation." He paused for a beat. "That's all."

In the car, the sergeant asked him for an explanation of the last exchange with Gatta Mignon.

"You shocked me, Liguori."

"Sure, but why? Marialuigia Moreno neither has the concert nor is she disconcerted, she's done. She gave me the idea of someone who's taken so many kicks in the ass and the teeth that even if she was willing to take more, she simply wouldn't have any place to put them. What do you think about her?"

"She's remarkably skilled in her use of words, she talks straight, but not because she's bringing who knows what truth along with her, like anyone else, for that matter: it's just that while she's thinking, she can draw on authentic sentiments."

"She's a True Artist. Like Giuseppe Càrita."

49.

Darkness was our daily bread, or actually it was yours. And it was no accident that you stumbled upon it.

You used darkness for other purposes too, when you felt any kind of malaise before a show, or when your memories were scraping their fingernails across the blackboard of your skull and sleep wouldn't come, after the cornucopia of chemicals.

Sleep. I never stayed with you, afterward. Never. I did what you wanted and then you'd send me away. Not even once did I see you sleep through the night.

I could hear you while you told other people: I have to turn it all off, even the little red light on the television, which gives me a pain right here, you get it? Right here. I still didn't sleep, but at least the brain stoned out on total darkness. The dark is good for gastritis, sudden hoarseness, and other problems as well.

You laughed and talked dirty. But I know how to talk dirty better than you did, in a whisper or in a scream, the way you liked it.

Then, in the darkness, you'd bless me between one insult and the next: you're a handsome devil, you have a perennial blaze crackling in your chest. Your mouth spits out gold and sea salt.

Because you have a way all your own of blending disgust and thirst-quenching water, so that it only makes you thirstier still.

You've addled my sense of time, I don't know anymore whether you were or you are.

It's such an enormous abuse to modify a person's perception of the minutes, the hours, the years.

When you're with me that's what happens.

This thing with time is a curse, yet another masquerade of which you are, or you were, a master.

I never told you this, but everything I did "during" was also because I hoped that it might change the "after."

It never did a bit of good, you always dismissed me lovingly with a: Now run along. Disappear, and I mean it, and not only into the darkness.

Now, yes, I've seen you sleeping an enduring sleep, while sucking on grass. No, that's not right, this time too I had to go away.

50

Liguori walked into Martusciello's office, visibly on edge.

The captain was delighted to see the roles reversed: for once, he was the calm one, and the detective was upset. He went on shuffling papers. He'd gathered documents on investigations having to do with illegal betting and related activities: false bets, money laundering, artificially hedged bets, commercial fraud, blackmail, extortions, false front companies, and lots more. The quantity of numbers, conclusions, and reports were filling his head, so his indifference to the detective's presence came across as convincing.

Liguori started in with a succession of objections, Martusciello talked with his head down, as he was leafing through the documents.

"I'm pleased. It's so rare that you openly lose your temper, without the twists and turns that you know how to execute so well. You've changed, Liguori, there's a new soul in you, with the price sticker still dangling on a string. Bravo. Something's different, what could it be? Do you have a girlfriend? Come, come, gallant knight, open your heart, loosen the bridle of the horse you don't have and ride toward new worlds."

"Martusciello, cut it out. Why didn't you tell me that Marialuigia Moreno had violated the judicial seals? For what goddamned reason on earth would you not keep me up-to-date on all the details of the case? And look me in the eye."

Martusciello ignored the request and kept his eyes focused on the documents.

"What can I tell you, Liguori, since your point of reference is Malanò, it didn't strike me as necessarily the best idea. Understandably."

"I'm not even going to dignify that with a response."

"No question, you've changed. Verona did you good."

Carità rudely shoved open the door and the man he had with him. Martusciello and Liguori were astonished: Carità had been a mild-mannered person even before the courses in acting and speech that had caused his condescension to degenerate into pedantry.

Martusciello finally looked up from his desk and took off his glasses.

"What's this, Peppino?"

Carità forgot his correct pronunciation and carefully gauged movements: he forced the man down in a chair and reported to his superior officers, in thick dialect, that he had brought Menico Gargiulo into the police station because, passing himself off as a taxi driver, he had defrauded a number of passengers with the old five-euro con game. Every time one of his passengers offered to pay with a fifty-euro bill, he'd sneakily exchange it for a five-euro note and tell the passenger they must be mistaken. If the unfortunate victim tried to object, he'd threaten them.

"And that's nothing," Carità concluded. "Do you want to know who he tried to pull the con job on this time, right outside, near the ferryboats for Procida? The wonderful actress Santina D'Offerta. It's just crazy, nobody has any respect anymore. Not even for True Art."

Martusciello carefully observed the fat man, who seemed much more concerned about his gastric disturbances than Carità's accusations.

"Ah, so that's the reason for your indignation. And where is the victim of this outrage?"

"Santina D'Offerta is talking to Blanca Occhiuzzi, I accompanied her personally."

Liguori left for the RAI Auditorium.

51.

Blanca couldn't figure out why Santina D'Offerta was so upset. It struck her as excessive: after all Carità had intervened in a timely fashion and the actress had recovered her money. But she kept pitching her voice in a vibrato of anxiety that struck Blanca as contrived.

After filing her complaint, the woman asked about Liguori. She said that she'd met him a few days ago, at one of her performances.

Blanca, pretending further curiosity, asked her the date of the performance, then she walked the woman over to Liguori's office, but he'd already left.

As she said goodbye to the woman, Blanca caught a whiff of the vanilla scent on her skin, caramel mouth, patchouli hands, bergamot and cedar hair. The coincidence between preparations for Verona and the birth of this new friendship between the actress and Liguori fit between a fragrance whose brand she recognized and annoyance. Jealousy loosed with a laugh that revealed rotten teeth.

The depression that ensued suggested to Blanca the precarious nature of her own exoticism and the durability of the actress's oriental perfumes.

She searched for the missing piece of her defense, tossed into a forgotten corner of her head the heels on which she'd teetered at the cliff's edge, and went on working.

Her new telephone alerted her in a soft murmured message that Nini would be getting out of school early today. Blanca remembered the hasty sound of her daughter's bare feet scampering through the apartment.

Liguori imagined the conversation between Santina D'Offerta and Blanca. If he'd been on edge before, it only grew worse.

The last thing on earth you need to worry about is protecting yourself from me. Ridiculous, he thought. He parked outside the Polytechnic and looked up at the mosaic along the base of the building. He'd gone by it a hundred times without ever stopping to decipher the figures. The blur of colors, with a prevalence of watery blue-green, took on the significance in the detective's eyes that he chose to assign to it: a celebration of human progress. The building and the progress concealed from view the public housing and part of Viale Augusto and its colonial architecture.

Liguori headed off on foot toward RAI's regional headquarters in the Via Marconi, leaving behind him a tangle of developments, of crusades with shields held high in defense of nothing in particular, of palm trees uprooted and then replanted in an alternation of urban design close to his own useless thoughts.

In response came his usual urge to find the logic of events guided by others and hence the determination to uncover something about the concert recording that he couldn't seem to find.

The girl at the security desk recognized him. Liguori had been to RAI headquarters before:

"These visits are turning into a habit, Detective."

"I come just to see you."

"That strikes me as the only possible explanation: there's practically no one else here today."

Liguori didn't take the elevator, he headed up the stairs determined to visit every floor, if nothing else for an excursion.

After the first flight of stairs, he went into a seventies-look-ing room, took a seat, and at his leisure studied a studio upright piano, the microphone, nicely undulating moldings, lines from the years of his youth.

A man stuck his head out of the glass director's booth:

"Are you looking for someone?"

"Maybe you. I'm Detective Liguori of the Pozzuoli police station. I'm trying to find the recording of Jerry Vialdi's last concert."

The man introduced himself, and Liguori noticed, more than the name, the courteous manner and the seventies jacket. Perhaps the sound technician had never left his booth.

"I'm very sorry, but I'm not sure I can be of any help to you. I'm in charge of regional radio broadcasts."

"There's one thing you can tell me anyway: in your opinion, what could happen to the recording of a concert? Is it possible that it was put away somewhere, or that it got lost?"

"In the case of the concert you're referring to, the structure merely hosted the show, while the organizers and technicians were non-staff. And in any case I doubt that any recordings are likely to be lost. You know, the amount of work that goes into it, the money and the time, you wouldn't want to throw it away."

"Even if it turned out badly?"

"What was it for?"

"A live album."

"Well, it depends, if the recording has already been done and there are problems, I guess you might throw it away, but I'd imagine only once you were done with the editing, once the work was complete. It would seem stupid to get rid of it before then."

"How long have you been working here?"

"Since 1978. Just think, I myself recently had to hunt for old tapes from years gone by for a radio montage they were editing."

"Thanks." The detective was reminded of the antiwar collages, ferociously naïve, that he put together in his first year at university for student protests. Likewise the same age as the furnishings and the technician's jacket.

The quirk in Liguori's head took up permanent residence: he needed to find out who had destroyed or concealed that recording and, above all, why.

52

Martusciello remained in his office with the cabbie and Carità; he took Menico Gargiulo's ID and turned his back to the window, to get better light, so he could read the details and get a clearer view of the picture.

He laughed, this snapshot bore no relationship to the face of the man sitting across from him. From the driver's license came the smile of a fair-haired young man in his early twenties, with light-colored eyes.

"Why, you should have told me that you were Prince Charming in your younger years! What the hell do you think you're doing? Put that down immediately." He glared at Carità. "Weren't you going to say anything?"

"Forgive me, Captain, I thought he was reading his own papers, to sign them." Menico Gargiulo had picked up a sheet of paper from Martusciello's desk, and was still reading.

"Now, don't get bent out of shape, everyone knows what's written here. It's Pulcinella's secret," he concluded, using the Neapolitan term for an open secret.

"Gargiulo, have you mistaken police reports and transcripts of depositions for magazines to leaf through in a waiting room? And what do you mean by 'everyone knows what's written here'?"

"That is what I mean. If I explain Pulcinella's secret then you'll let me go? I'll give you a nice quick overview of all these papers, it'll save you lots of time."

"Tell us and then we'll decide."

"You start with the minor leagues, it's better, it's easier. The players get smaller salaries so the money they're paid to throw the games is more attractive. Which is to say, it makes a bigger impression. Plus in the minor leagues the kicking is bad, the brawls after the matches too, so your career isn't going to last as long. The gentlemen in the betting parlors, which are now legal, have two sections: one people know about, and one people don't know about. Right?"

"One that's legal and one that's illegal," Carità translated, clearly enunciating the final l's.

"I didn't speak to you, and I wouldn't if you paid me."

"Drop dead," Carità replied, losing his impeccable diction in the process. Martusciello put an end to the exchange.

"Go on, Gargiulo."

"Now then, hunger can bring on a nastier kind of hunger, and so people start climbing the ladder. They move into higher markets. Notice this detail: only some, because the ones who are specialized in the minor leagues stay there, and if you ask me, that's a smart move because they're not as likely to get caught. Certain others might climb the ladder: Series B, Series A. The game works in exactly the same way. The gentlemen who run the parlors take the bets, and they especially take them in large number for certain matches. They take them regulation and they take them secret, illegal, however you call them. They take advantage of the addiction of sports fans: Atalanta wins and wins; Roma wins and wins; Chievo wins and wins; Cremonese wins and wins; Bari wins and wins; Como wins and wins; Bologna wins and wins; Ascoli wins and wins; Juve wins and wins. And so on. The names of the teams I just mentioned, Captain, are taken at random, the first names that came into my head from the Panini soccer cards album from when I was just a tyke. So let's say that the owners take in two or three million euros per parlor on the victory that is supposed to come from the team they love best, or even more, I'm just giving examples. At this point they contact the players that we already know about, better yet, the strikers, all you need is three good players, maybe the goalie could be the wild card. They pay and the players arrange for a tie, let's say. The gambling parlors take in the money plus they have the advantage of a nice little money laundering operation, with the money from neighboring business sectors: loan-sharking, shakedowns and protection, drugs, arms, and things like that, and then they invest that money in other businesses. Have I made myself clear?"

"Perfectly." Martusciello looked around for his lighter.

"And I know that, in particular, you already know all about this whole thing. Now you tell me: how could it be that a fake taxi driver like me, who barely makes end meet with a few pennies picked up in out-of-the-way corners of the city . . . "

"A few pennies?" Carità blurted out. "You pick up in a year the retirement fund that I'll never see!"

"I didn't speak to you, and I already told you I wouldn't, you have nasty manners."

"Go on, Gargiulo." Martusciello took the first puff, the best of all.

"Now, how could it be that a flea like me knows all this and you don't? The truth is that you know it too, and you're content, even, that the industry can't be stopped. Factories can shut down, the world economy is such a fucking mess that even the biggest sharks are eating each other alive, the only decent source of revenue left is soccer. And wherever you find profits you're going to find hungry crows. Let's just say that the crows are the melancholy cost of doing business." Martusciello put out his cigarette in the triangular Pepsi ashtray, which followed him from office to office along with his Bakelite telephone.

"We know it, you claim. Fine. Still, we need the criminal complaints, the statements. Now Carità is going to be so good as to draw up a regular police report of your admirably detailed testimony and you're going to sign it for us."

"As you like, but then we're going to say goodbye and we're friends as before." Martusciello lowered his chin just once. Carità was overwhelmed with astonishment.

"Really?"

"Really." Menico Gargiulo signed his named with a final self-satisfied *o*.

Carità extended his hand and accompanied him to the door, which he closed carefully with a certain respect.

"Captain, I would never have expected this honorable behavior from the taxi driver."

"Fake taxi, fake license plate, fake driver's license, super-fake photograph on a fake driver's license. Fake name. The honorary signature didn't even cost him a penny's worth of risk."

"So why did you let him go?"

"Because his account is believable, at least in part, and it's useful to me."

"I'll never understand you, Captain."

"Or I you. It's why we love each other."

53.

I told you it wasn't right. You grabbed me by the back of my neck and bent me over until you were shoving my head against my knees.

You don't know a thing and you can't understand what's right. You, of all people. That's what you said.

From that position I went on talking, with that child's voice you like so much. Trying to calm you down. Trying to tell you what I really thought.

Tell me that you love me. I was thinking.

Your hand was caressing the hairline at the nape of my neck.

Let me try, father, don't spoil my chances in advance. Everything becomes impossible, even love, even anger. Everything. Even laughter starts to take on the sound of a slap.

I am the hand that pitches the billiard ball that can either bounce off the green felt table or not. I'm the attempt, the endeavor. Listen to the lovely sound of the word. En-dea-vor.

Tell me that you love me. I was thinking.

The opportunities have already been compromised by another case whose rules are unknown to us. At least here, in this garden of days, we try as best we can, we dare, we lose, we get back on our feet. Listen to the sound of the sea: we don't know how much longer the waves will roll in calm and unhurried. And the air that comes in from outside, in spite of the closed window, that still finds its way through some unsuspected fissure.

Tell me that you love me. I was thinking.

I'm your son, let me try to guess, and give me the slightest window of victory. Let me be sincere, nasty, bold.

Tell me that you love me. I was thinking.

Even your success would have been wonderful if you hadn't been elevated on high by hands that were so evil, so harsh, hands that demanded their price while they were making you rich.

Tell me that you love me. I was thinking.

Instead you flew into another one of your animal rages again.

There I am, as you bang my head against my knees again, slowly, slowly. Then your own anger starts to excite you and you accentuate the movement.

You see that you don't know a thing? They came to get me while I was singing in front of the rigid tulle tutu of that hateful little girl and they told me thus and such. What could I do, my dear young scientist? I said no thanks, you can have someone else climb onto your parade float, celebrate the triumph of some other idiot. What would it have changed? Nothing. And when I plump myself down right in the middle of the Posillipo bleachers, when I suck the pure gold of American music, when I grab the woman I chose or else your own misery, I don't think to myself that I was dealt a bum hand. I think of four of a kind, a hand full of aces of hearts. And that's fine.

Tell me that you love me.

You laughed your usual slap and we started.

I didn't tell you that knowing the end, having the answers at your disposal, would do nothing to save your life.

54

Turn it off, Sergio."

"I put on your favorite Mozart and you don't appreciate it."

"No, I don't appreciate it, turn it off."

"You're a lunatic."

Blanca lifted her head in search of the lunatic's moon, looking for the light that never came.

As she walked toward her own front door she enjoyed the breath that separated her from tranquility. She wanted, that night more than any other, to escape the outside world, relax her vigilant attention to her footsteps and conceal herself in her unrestrained gestures. She wanted an indifferent sense of hearing and careless hands and rapid feet to recognize the domesticated space of a familiar routine.

No matter how eager she was to be home, she still sensed something out of the ordinary, even as she was turning the key in the lock. She stopped and moved her hands down the surface of the door, between the lock and the doorjamb she felt faint scratches on the smooth wooden finish.

She went up one flight and phoned Nini.

"Where are you?"

"I'm down at Sergio's, I forgot my keys and I came over to get his, but he's not answering his buzzer."

"He was with me, he'll be there any minute. Wait for him, then stay at his place and tell him to come join me upstairs on the landing outside our apartment. Tell him to take the elevator, not to use the stairs."

"Why?"

Blanca cut off the call and stood there, motionless, counting off the minutes. The noise of the old motor grinding with the effort of hoisting the elevator car up the shaft calmed her.

She told Sergio that it was possible that someone had broken into the apartment.

The key turned in the lock, making only one click. Not double-bolted. The door swung open.

"Tell me what you see, but don't go in."

"It's a shambles. There's broken glass everywhere and all the furniture's been shoved out of place, clothing; it's messier in there than even my apartment's ever been. What should we do?"

Blanca called the police station and told them what had happened.

Martusciello and Liguori came right over. Before determining the quantity and more importantly the quality of the damage, the captain summoned the forensics team. While they were waiting, Blanca told them that probably they'd find the same nothing they found in the sheet metal shed, then she felt suddenly exhausted and hopeless.

"Sergio, take me to Nini."

Before she left, Liguori took her aside with some excuse. He took her hand, turned it over, and kissed the inside of her wrist.

While the officers of the forensics team were working with Martusciello and Liguori to develop an initial report on their inspection, Captain Malanò arrived.

"Welcome to my house," he said.

"Thanks," Martusciello replied. "Go on working, men."

"Captain, we haven't found any of the usual evidence you'd find in an apartment burglary. We did find signs of an atypical carefulness on the part of the burglar, even though the damage is quite visible, and whether or not Occhiuzzi tells us that valuable objects have been stolen."

Malanò really did feel at home there, after all his police station was just a short walk from Blanca's apartment building.

" . . . and even though just yesterday another apartment in the area was broken into and even though we receive reports of apartment burglaries every week and even though and even though."

"Is this a problem for you?" Martusciello asked. "No, I mean, is this a problem for you that the officers doing the investigation voice doubts that strike me as reasonable?"

"No, doubts are perfectly healthy in the work that we do. It's fixations that I can't stand."

"Oh, I can't stand them either, especially if it's a serial killer hunting mastiff that's got its teeth into something and just won't let go. By the way, Grimaldi told me that he gave you his findings from Vialdi's autopsy: the cause of death was myocardial infarction."

Liguori intervened.

"This apartment is the one place where a partially blind woman can feel that she's safe. You never thought of that. What astonishes me is the way you keep tugging on the rope of a completely different investigation, when a valued colleague of ours has just suffered a profound violation of what little peace life affords her. I'm in complete agreement with the conclusions that Martusciello has not yet laid out explicitly, it's quite likely that this burglary is in some way linked to the Vialdi case. Which only makes it worse, because once again Blanca Occhiuzzi stands to lose a substantial part of her hard-won equilibrium at the service of a civil and investigative community that might not even deserve the efforts of those who possess eyes to see with. I'm leaving." The officers of the forensic team trooped out behind Liguori.

Malanò extended his hand to Martusciello.

"The two of us will talk again. My compliments to your men, they have original ideas about bureaucratic hierarchies and objective facts."

Martusciello felt a flush of contentment. The summer was finally over.

"Well, one thing's certain, you know how to put together a compliment, there aren't a lot of police officers like Occhiuzzi and Liguori."

55

Blanca sat trembling on the sofa, next to Nini. This wasn't like her. She decided that, if she went on doing things that she didn't feel she had any right to do, her universe would turn head-over-heels and she'd plummet headlong into the sky.

Nini caressed her hand:

"I don't want this to turn into a habit. I'm the daughter here."

"I heard you when you were talking to Tita and called me your mother."

"Why am I not surprised? You hear everything."

"When I can't go on but I have to go on, I make use of the following exercise: I order my thoughts to go take a rest, a sort of labor of love. The stupid advantage of a limitation, which it would be best in any case not to have. I'm accustomed to husbanding my strength: I'm going to need it the next time I stumble, guaranteed to be soon. Or else, I have no time to waste, I can't say which. Half an hour of pain is sufficient, a rapid blenderful of a dozen or so tablespoonsful is more than enough. And after all, what do you know, even joy has its shortcomings. Often it trips me up, makes me think I could even see the moon or what the hell else, I don't know. So stupid. Voices betray me less often, yours, when you were talking with Tita, even gave me an extra supply of courage. I'd like to train you to recognize them, I certainly understand that I learned out of necessity, but if I could teach you to decipher the sentiments of sounds, my misfortune might serve a useful purpose. Because we need to do it, Nini, we have to protect ourselves and translate the damage, otherwise the imperfections will win, until they make us enjoy a pain we never asked for."

"You're preaching now, you've turned back into a mother. What were they looking for, Blanca?"

"I don't know. I'm racking my brains to figure it out. We don't have anything at home that's important enough to justify this much work and anyone who knows how to work at this level is well aware of exactly what they're looking for."

Sergio knocked at the door of his own bedroom.

"The detective is here and he wants to talk to you."

"Let him in." Nini started to get up from the sofa. "No, stay here."

Liguori didn't look like himself either.

"How are you? No, I imagine that you're fine, all things considered." He broke off. "No real damage, and no one was home when they . . . " He broke off again. "But I also thought that you . . . " He broke off for the third time. "In other words, that you . . . " The detective wasn't accustomed to this kind of awkwardness, and he didn't know how to dilute it into a flow of words.

"Thanks for coming." Blanca came back to the recent events in order to help the man get free of his overwhelming embarrassment. "Nini and I were just wondering what they might have been looking for."

Liguori recovered.

"Did you bring home documents, police reports, wiretaps or recordings, or any other material that might be of interest to anyone?"

"No."

"Do you generally record notes or other information on the cases you're working on?"

"My memory is adequate, even excessive at times."

"Did you receive any mail, say from Verona, just as a for instance? Did Adami send you anything?"

"Nothing, I get all my mail at the office."

Nini stood up from the couch to pull a receipt out of the pocket of her tight jeans.

"No, that's not true, you got this. I forgot to give it to you."

56

The morning subway had become a train again. The change, apparently irrelevant, was a sort of resurrection for Martusciello. The passengers with faces puffy from sleep had become travelers again, they could still take part in any given surprise, however passively.

"Swings don't have a future, trains do," he murmured toward the hat on the head of the woman with sad eyes who'd managed to find a seat for her morning commute. "Because, you see, my dear sad woman, swings come and go, like trains, but they only cover a restricted, weary space. The future, on the other hand, as far as I'm concerned, must have a certain margin for derailing from the obvious, the future must be familiar with the word despite. Despite the tricks, the denials, the slabs of asbestos, the betrayals performed and suffered, the deaths, the social climbers and their sharp elbows, despite a time that refuses to bring us old age, despite a vast array of out-rages. Every so often, my dear woman, a *despite* breaks free and establishes itself. It climbs down off the swing and catches a train. What I feel isn't exactly hope, no, rather I would call it surprise, a jack-in-the-box that springs out of its box and goes cuckoo peekaboo: *I am* in spite of everything.

"And then there's the issue of Liguori," he whispered to the same woman who was looking out at the sea with an indignant expression, just catching sight of it as it appeared from behind the ugly buildings, still steel-mill black. "I still confuse work and friendship. This has brought me certain disadvantages, but if I've failed to correct this bad habit before now, it's at least worth my while to take the good with the bad when I realize that I wasn't entirely wrong when I sensed that there was someone on my side. For once, the horseman climbed onto his horse, shoved the motorcyclist and my doubts aside, and went."

He put off his arrival back at the police station. In order to celebrate in his manner the enchantment that had turned the subway into a train, he went to the terrace of Villa Avellino. He walked through the park, remembering Liguori's long diatribes about the Roman cistern incorporated into the villa. After his transfer to the Pozzuoli police station the two men frequently met there.

He breathed in the salt air that was wafting up to embrace the citrus trees in order to rid itself of a majestic odor, disturbed, but only to a certain extent, by the sulfurous wind coming from the Solfatara.

"I've always said: stench mixes with perfume. And that's the way it is."

Carità was waiting for him at the front door of the police station.

"You're late."

"Did we have an appointment?"

"Not with me, Captain, but there's an important lawyer upstairs waiting to see you, Luigi D'Amore." Martusciello wondered how his newly rediscovered reluctance had managed to invade new territories, this wasn't the first time that it had happened to him and in this circumstance, too, he could think of no answers. D'Amore had bothered to come in first thing in the morning, and that struck him as a good sign.

"Explain it to me clearly, is he important because he's a lawyer or why?"

"Captain, why don't you explain to me: what exactly do you seem to find that I ought to be saying to you?"

"Carità, I hear with pleasure that you're bringing back your good old tangled grammar."

"Of course I have, you told me that you were going to have me transferred. What a disgraceful thing to say, with all due respect. No one but you knows that I have two different families on two different floors of the same apartment building. In spite of this, you've told me that you're going to have me sent away. What are they going to do without me?"

The deputy, during the same case that had brought Blanca and Nini together, had revealed to Martusciello, and to Martusciello alone, that he had, along with his own children by his wife, another child with another woman; the woman's husband had left for reasons that had nothing to do with her betrayal and so Carità now found himself managing an intricate situation, unaccustomed and delicate, with an extended family on two different landings of the same stairwell.

"Well, what are they going to do! What do they do now, Peppino. The salary would be the same even if they transfer you to a different region. This may have escaped you, but we still live in Italy. Leaving aside the stew, of course."

"You woke up in a good mood this morning, I'm happy to see it. Well, why don't you go upstairs, the important lawyer is still waiting for you."

"You still haven't told me why he's important."

"Let's just say this: he's not important. He's a lawyer, period. In fact, he's not even a lawyer. Captain, there's a certain Luigi D'Amore waiting for you in your office."

"In my office?" Martusciello tried to remember whether he'd taken the keys out of the lock in his desk drawer. "Just why did you let him into my office? Wasn't the waiting room good enough for him? Oh, wait, I almost forgot, he's an important gentleman. When will we down here in the Kingdom of Naples ever get rid of our collective inferiority complex, I wonder."

"Captain, I wish the best of health to you and to the thousand questions that you ask: but why are you so damned insidious when there's joy in your heart?"

57

While Martusciello contemplated the transformation of the subway into a train, Liguori was waiting for Blanca downstairs from Sergio's apartment.

In the car, they didn't talk about what they'd be likely to find. Liguori and Nini had studied the receipt down to the finest detail and they had made all conjectures imaginable. There was nothing left to do but wait.

The detective looked at the woman in the bright morning sunlight: Blanca hadn't slept well, and the skin of her face, even paler than usual, let the network of veins beneath show through. Her movements had lost all sense of harmony, deprived as she was of much needed rest in a domestic environment; and Blanca showed, with her seeking hands, the darkness that at other times she so adroitly concealed.

"I'm tired."

"You're just as pretty as ever," Liguori said, more to himself than to her.

They stood in line outside the locked doors of the postal office. Behind them extended a line of elderly people who looked as if they were waiting for a bus to come take them on a field trip. Even the grumbling about waiting in line rang with sounds of a greeting.

Liguori led Blanca past the sliding doors. They walked up to the service window and presented the receipt. They managed to resist the urge to open the package they'd just been given.

They went to Liguori's apartment. Blanca, despite her

impatience, familiarized herself with odors she'd never forget: the scent of Gay-Odin chocolate, antique wood, musk, tuberose, and dust, lots and lots of dust.

"You don't open your windows much, do you?"

"There's not a lot of fresh air in Piazza Sannazzaro. Maybe at night, when the traffic from the grotto quietens down."

They sat down on a couple of chairs overlooking the sea that was invisible to Blanca. The detective slipped on a pair of thin gloves and opened the package, taking care not to rip the wrapping paper, and lifted like a belated trophy the recording of Vialdi's last concert. The dedication read *To my Julia, whom I adore, Gennaro.*

"While I was driving myself crazy to find it, this damned thing was fast asleep, waiting for us just a short walk from the police station. Thanks to Nini. It was mailed from the post office closest to the Piazza Garibaldi train station."

"Listen, we should just be grateful that Nini didn't lose the receipt. Organization isn't her strong suit. Julia Marin must have mailed it to me just before catching her train back to Verona. Before going to meet her death at the Bentegodi stadium. 'Or else I'll surprise you, who can say?' is what she said to me during our first and only conversation. She surprised me all right, and how. There are so many things I wish I could ask her. I wish I could talk to her."

"That won't be possible. Now we can only listen."

"We'll listen to it the first time together, then I'm going to need some suitable headphones."

"All I have are these MP3 earbuds."

"They may not be particularly suitable, but my good ones are buried under the rubble."

The recording was of poor quality, and certainly justified the idea that someone had judged it inadequate for selections for a live album.

Liguori came away with nothing, except for the clear idea that he'd never buy the record.

Blanca was transformed, her complexion shifted to a light pink hue, her movements once again came to match her intentions. Toward the end of the recording, she froze.

"Go back a minute." Liguori did as he was asked, for all the "agains" that followed.

It seemed to the detective that Blanca was interested in a meaningless detail. At the end of the concert, a male voice asked Vialdi: *He's waiting for you, do you want me to talk to him?* And Vialdi replied: *Gigi, be a good boy, you know that after the concert I always want to be alone.*

Blanca slipped the earbuds into her ears, let Liguori's hand guide hers to the controls, and sat there in a state of enchantment deciphering something that struck her as impossible.

58.

Counselor Luigi D'Amore welcomed Martusciello as if he hadn't been waiting for him to arrive for close to two hours.

"I wonder if this guy takes that smile off at least to go to sleep," the captain thought, then picked one of his own that didn't turn out very well. "*Buon giorno*, Counselor, you came to call on me earlier than expected."

"*Buon giorno*, Captain, I imagine you're referring to the time of morning. I know that you're an early riser in terms of your arrival in the office, so I chose to come a little beforehand, but I haven't been waiting long. Even though I'm hardly a slave to duty, I do have office hours to keep, hence the haste."

"I was referring to the date, we only met recently."

"I wanted to inform you that after our recent chat I went over the documentation of my client, Jerry Vialdi, with some care, and I happened to notice a number of notable variations in terms of his personal wealth."

"Ex-client, Counselor, but I'm sure Vialdi will forgive the mistake: the dead are very even-tempered."

"I wouldn't know. I was just saying that, even as you keep front and center the important lead of a serial killer, perhaps it's possible to extend your line of investigation to include a likely extortion."

"Explain this to me clearly: you're saying that you'd noticed that your client's accounts were seesawing in a way that you found inexplicable?"

"That's exactly right, Captain."

"Damn, better than a CPA!"

"Captain, I was responsible for all the interests of my ex-client."

"I understand. So you believe that the victim was laying out substantial sums for what would appear to have been a case of blackmail."

"I can even tell you more about that: there had been a lawsuit underway for plagiarism, then the recording company that was bringing the suit decided to withdraw it. That's as far as the courts are concerned, more than that I couldn't say."

"That's right, the dead don't hold grudges. I thank you for this spontaneous offer of information, which by the way opens a whole new calzone that has nothing to do with me; I would invite you to report this new information to Captain Malanò, who I feel sure will be appreciative. For the moment, I'm looking into a burglary. You know, a small crew of professional thieves broke into the apartment of Sergeant Blanca Occhiuzzi and wrecked the place. This slap in the face of a close colleague, legally blind, by the way, really ticked me off, so let me assure you that I will neither sleep nor rest until I track down the guilty parties, who of course had nothing to do with the death or your client." He gave Luigi D'Amore a long hard stare. "Or am I wrong?"

It dawned on the lawyer that Martusciello was less of a village donkey than rumor would have it. The captain was either offering him a deal or laying a trap for him.

"And you want me to tell you?"

"Yes, I prefer to determine myself the terms of any bartering that may take place."

Martusciello was left alone to ponder the conversation that had just taken place. He told himself that they must have something that they didn't realize they even had. That must be the explanation: otherwise the lawyer would never have put the information about Vialdi's personal wealth on display, nor would he have tried to draw attention to an extortion attempt that made no sense whatsoever.

59

On the other hand, killing you was simply dictated by circumstances, my dear lady. A whirlwind already set spinning, a slight shortness of breath after a long run.

No amorous wrath for you.

I *never* could stand your benign calm, you accepted your jailer's infamous words and turned them into a lullaby.

All the same, your young teacher of wicked hopes never spared you the infliction of his wounds, it's just that before his eyes you broke them down and turned them into slight misdemeanors, sheer momentary distractions from a higher good.

You beautified a poverty-stricken landscape, every encounter for you was beautiful. Simply beautiful.

You stripped away the foliage of his mistreatment the way you might with a vegetable. You told me that yourself. So long, betrayals, insults, small-time annoyances, goodbye as well to the distasteful depth of lies, abuses, and crimes. So long, insults, certainly less than what he had offered me. What remained to you was the little jewel of the juicy flesh, and you swallowed it, letting him know that that was the only meal he had ever offered to you.

And he believed you.

I *was* following you and the other idiot who was following behind the two of you. Just think of it, it's almost funny: a two-bit parade. Jerry and Julia, a couple off the top of a wedding cake, Maria Datri, the mother of a none-too-numerous family, chasing after you, and me bringing up the rear of the procession.

When Signora Julia Marin phoned me to blackmail me with the fine manners that she had in her voice, I was at the station soon afterward.

My dear, it never occurred to you that I was on the same train as you, looking out at the same landscape, waiting to get to the same stop as you. I didn't even need to force you to come with me, you were looking for death in a vague promise.

Maybe while you were coming with me and waiting for me to get rid of the security guards, you sat there like a good little girl, and you cleaned off the nasty leaves from your last few breaths before dying.

You told me that you knew. Ah, what a painful stab in the heart, what an affront! You told me that he talked to you about me. And about the other women. You didn't care a bit, while the two of you were together you were just the two of you, you were sure of it, because you alone let him give birth, in the midst of all the pus of infected placenta, to his true, beautiful soul. You laughed: even you have a beautiful soul, too bad no one will help you find it.

You told me that while you were making love, he looked you in the face and looked at you moaning, caressing your neck and your mouth. That's exactly what you said.

He spoke to you of love.

In the perfect, diffuse lighting that he insisted on to keep from insulting your age.

Before I put you to sleep with the same sedatives I used on the security guards you also told me that they were going to catch me, that you'd mailed the blind woman the recording of the concert. But it was too late and I completed my project.

It was neither a relief nor a pity to me when I killed you. He was already dead, it didn't change a thing.

60

Martusciello had noticed that certain days, after starting out almost nicely, gradually gained confidence with the hours, boasting the benefit of a good start and really never stopping.

This was that kind of day.

After bidding farewell to Luigi D'Amore, he suddenly felt the urge to invite everyone involved in the Vialdi case to come into the police station for a chat. He knew in advance that this probably wouldn't add any information to what he already knew, but the mechanisms of understanding that worked for him demanded a sort of cataloguing in person. The results of the depositions weren't really all that important after all.

"I come from the era of paper, pen, and wasted time. And that's that," he said to himself.

All he asked Maria Datri about was her daughter, how school was going for her, how she was growing up, and her friendship with Nini. The woman displayed astonishment at these questions that ranged so far afield of what she was expecting, but she also felt relief at the shift. The captain had given her back what she had once had, he had taken away a painful slice of her life. There still remained others, substantial and meaningful, but concerning them she'd continue to remain as silent as she had over the previous years and years.

Rosina Mastriani emphatically expressed her gratitude to the police force as a whole, though she then specified that she felt gratitude to Liguori in particular, for having bought a car from her that she could no longer afford, for finding her a job that she described as "finally difficult," and for helping her to patch things up with her children. She talked about forgiveness worse than any priest.

Mara Scacchi answered apathetically, eyes half closed. She had replaced her amorous despondency with a chemically induced slough, and perhaps they both coexisted when Vialdi was still alive. Martusciello considered that at least the woman had no need of a dealer; she could do her dope shopping right there at home. She regained a little vigor only when she started to complain about the press which had already tried her and found her guilty, then she slipped back into her indifference, eyes open wide, staring into nothingness. Before leaving, her voice took on a prophetic tone and announced an impending confession. Martusciello attributed her mysticism to pills.

While the captain was questioning Marialuigia Moreno the phone call from Funicella Corta arrived. Sconciglio wished to inform the Captain, through Funicella Corta, that the lawyer was a whore and had completely slipped his leash.

Martusciello said only:

"So you're back from Marseilles, the number you're calling from is your regular number once again."

He resumed at an intentional distance his dialogue with Gatta Mignon. The woman was surprisingly lucid, and once again was successful at shifting the line of questioning as if she were running the interview. She reprised the same arguments as in previous sessions, in the exact same words. Martusciello didn't like the echo and summoned Carità.

"Take the Signora downstairs, she has some statements to make about the violation of the judicial seals of the apartment of Gennaro Mangiavento, stage name Jerry Vialdi." Before they moved off, the captain explained to both of them with an abundance of details how deeply irritating, on the verge of causing him to vomit, he found the manipulative and instrumental use of people's artistic talents; the degree to which the ill concealed claims of superiority on the part of the learned intelligence and the jaded esthetics of those who felt they possessed God-given truths denied to the majority occupied completely different parts of the body's landscape as far as he was concerned. Moreover he cordially detested those who triggered in him pathetic surges of indignation unsuited to a man of his age and everything that he had seen and lived through.

Once the two had moved away he called back the confidential informant and brusquely instructed him on the fact that he had no intention of allowing himself to be used as a funnel for other people's overflow, even if the *other people* in question brought him, with FOB delivery at the police station, those responsible for the murders of Jerry Vialdi, Gioacchino Rizzo, and Julia Marin. And therefore, Signor Sconciglio and Funicella Corta, if they had any useful information about the case, should kindly do him the favor of using the classic channels of testimony and deposition. He concluded by emphasizing that the burglary at Casa Occhiuzzi had only helped him to dry up the last bit of patience that remained to him. As a result, the entire trade in information and tips had been shut down temporarily, due to a period of family mourning.

He felt better now.

61.

Martusciello had decided that he could consider his work day concluded, but that first he would toss onto Malanò's back the results of hours and hours spent questioning witnesses and climbing stairs.

"It's a paltry urge, a pastime for idiots. But I don't care, I just want to have a little fun," he told himself while waiting to be connected with his colleague. At last, he heard the voice he'd been waiting for. "I only wanted to have an idle chat with you, Malanò." He took his time explaining to him how many logical problems there were with the version of a serial murderer. Accompanied by the moans of boredom he could hear coming over the line, he organized the thoughts that he normally laid out in solitude. Reporting to him on the latest conversations he'd had with the informant and with Counselor Luigi D'Amore, he explained his suppositions: a singer attains success in part through murky connections; probably the cost of the favors received corresponded to a price in money laundering, various services, or perhaps just an array of useful contacts for illegal betting rings. At a certain point, this singer, having even received a certain education through the words and music of Gatta Mignon, starts creating problems. Martusciello said he was pretty sure that Vialdi's lawyer, Luigi D'Amore, would in the fullness of time confess as to the motive. He was a clever young operator, perfectly capable of evaluating costs and benefits. The death of the night watchman, the murder of Julia Marin, and the treasure hunt in the apartment of Martusciello's colleague all spoke eloquently of the consequences: something went wrong and, after all, the serial killer suit could have been stitched up a little more neatly. He wasn't going to rule out the possibility that private interests in Vialdi's chaotic life might have coincided with certain company interests.

"You like the manger scene, Malanò?"

"It's a lovely manger scene, too bad you're moving the shepherds yourself, without evidence, on the basis of theories that wouldn't stand up to a good hard spit. It's too late, Martusciello, go play by yourself."

"I was hoping I could make you happy, that's all. Kids who play cops and serial killers annoy the hell out of me. You're right, you can have more fun playing on your own."

The captain felt a certain sense of gratification in both feet and head, which were also linked by ties that surely existed but couldn't be proved.

Certainly, Malanò had a point, and he'd shaved some corners, in all likelihood the lawyer would stop delivering harangues in the police station, and all the uncertainties would remain uncertain.

Almost certainly they'd never find a guilty party for the murders, in keeping with a grim statistic on unsolved mortal tumults. He smiled. Perhaps he'd spoken to Malanò just to get in the last word. And that was enough to give Martusciello a dignified urge to go home.

He stood up, locked his desk drawer with the documents on illegal gambling, pulled the ancient shutters closed, and put on his jacket. That day of hours and hours had come to an end.

He was already heading for the door when Blanca and Liguori came through it.

The detective told Martusciello to hurry over to Blanca's office, there was something important they wanted him to hear.

The captain took off his jacket and followed the two of them.

They told him to sit at the sergeant's desk; she offered no advance explanation of the recording. The captain concentrated and listened, but didn't catch anything significant.

At that point, Liguori offered a chronicle of the final events, then isolated into a series of repetitions the minute that had so disconcerted Blanca, in an obsessive reprise of the phrases: *He's waiting for you, do you want me to talk to him? Gigi, be a good boy, you know that after the concert I always want to be alone.*

Martusciello continued not to understand.

"Did you think that Gigi might be Luigi D'Amore? That isn't him. I talked to him this morning, my recollection is fresh. This voice talking to Vialdi's voice doesn't belong to the lawyer. I've never heard it before."

Blanca was upset.

"It isn't possible that I'm the only one who recognizes that voice!"

Carità appeared before the three of them and said nothing in response to Liguori's comments concerning his irritating and intrusive timing.

The officer looked upset and vaguely absent, the hand that was clutching a sheet of paper was trembling slightly. He laid it down on Blanca's desk.

"It's not my fault, Captain," he murmured. "I hadn't understood a thing. There's no time."

Liguori and Martusciello rushed out into the street.

Carità read the contents of the sheet to Blanca, and heaved a lengthy sigh before the last sentence: *At least my suicide should be successful.*

"Well, I had understood, but it didn't serve any purpose."

62.

The terrace that had once belonged to Vialdi presented a scenario of destruction. The powerful gusting winds were tearing the last leaves off the branches, ripping them apart and bringing them together, tumbling in low whirlwinds with the remains of the other, already-fallen leaves. The sea was kicking up combative waves that crashed over the rocks and the narrow beach, invading the streets. As it pulled back to gather strength for each new assault, the water left patches of foam on the asphalt that remained alive, dissolving.

Marialuigia Moreno was standing on the furthest part of the terrace, the surface that jutted out past the railing. She was wearing a light white man's shirt, which hung on her small and ill-formed body like a dress.

Liguori moved off to summon help though without much hope of success: the gates enclosing the courtyards below would keep would-be rescuers from getting close enough and time was already running out.

Gatta Mignon's eyes were fixed on the patterns the sea foam made on the street below, she didn't turn around when the captain began to speak to her in the voice he used with his daughter.

"Stay in this misbegotten life."

"I came back to this misbegotten life, the wrong life. You know that, right, Captain? Seven lives as Gatta Mignon and seven deaths." Martusciello moved toward her with concealed motions, but Marialuigia Moreno saw him all the same.

"Don't you move, or I'll jump too early. The handsome detective may have gone to summon reinforcements, I like this American concert: I'll be able to throw myself into thin air in the presence of spectators."

"You could change. Maybe seven lives are too few." Passersby in the street began to gather, looking up at the terrace, sheltered from the sea that refused to rest its crashing waves.

"Not seven deaths. The first was when I saw him. The second was when he turned me into a child to be crucified, while I amused myself pounding nails into the wood all on my own. The third was when I helped him to steal from those who never forgive. The fourth was when I asked permission to kill someone who, in fact, hadn't forgiven. The fifth was when I hadn't known how to keep his death for myself. The sixth was when I set the table for death in the spread legs of Julia, someone who had the right to be looked in the face and talked to about love. The seventh was when I better understood what I already knew: the asphyxiating pain, which grabs you by the throat and chokes you with every breath, would never go away. I tried to hide, to come up with some remedy, to shuffle the cards, but the last con game failed to work out: I couldn't seem to fool myself. The eighth death will be the best." Reinforcements arrived with the noise of screeching tires, slamming doors, voices. The sea went on pounding.

Marialuigia Moreno turned toward Martusciello:

"A final performance for a nonpaying audience."

Her rapid plunge halted when she hit the iron bars, the metal pierced her short neck. Death, unlike love, had insisted on meeting her face to face.

Martusciello didn't stop to look at the corpse, instead he looked past the grey sheet metal that went on wobbling, on past the barrier, and looked at Nisida.

63

The world of written and verbal communications went wild. Liguori regained a number of years of his fictional youth that he'd lost during the summer. Martusciello asked his daughter to forgive him and she failed to understand why; feet and head elicited other days with their anarchy. Malanò distributed invitations to the press conference, headlined: *The Vialdi Case and the Suicide of the Serial Killer*. Carità stopped attending acting and diction courses. Rosina Mastriani suddenly felt lucky. Mara Scacchi kept gobbling down tablets. When Maria Datri heard about Marialuigia Moreno, she felt ashamed of her own petty gratification, but still went on luxuriating in it. Funicella Corta went back to Marseilles. The lawyer became a regular visitor to the Pozzuoli police station, first as a conscientious contributor to the investigations, and then when subpoenaed by the investigators.

Blanca withdrew for days into the apartment that now, thanks to Nini and Sergio, had been restored to order: she had only one voice to decipher.

Gatta Mignon had organized in her apartment a considerable quantity of notes, documents, invoices, gambling receipts, and statements.

She hadn't absolved herself, she hadn't forgiven.

The turnover of the holding companies behind the gambling ring reported back to an Asian main office, Jerry Vialdi was assigned to help the regional subsidiary with special bets; the Singing Maestro, available also for other services, bet huge sums on guaranteed outcomes, and then returned the take, neatly laundered with the illegal assistance of his lawyer. One time, he failed to give back.

Gatta Mignon had had to request permission to kill the singer. That permission had been gladly given, the subsidiary needed someone to hold responsible for the shortfall. They made a special request, however: could whoever did the job please distract the interest of the investigators with special effects worthy of a serial killer.

Marialuigia Moreno had said yes one last time.

The lawyer served Jerry Vialdi and his creditors, on alternating days. On the days when he was busily tending to the interests of his business rivals, he informed them of three (3) problems to solve:

the stadium night watchman might decide to open his mouth to speak at any moment, just as he had opened it to drink; it would be a problem to leave him free to say just who had plied him with bottles;

the lady from Verona no longer cared about going on living, therefore threats wouldn't be enough to shut her up;

what was needed was a nice thorough inspection of the sergeant's apartment. The recording had to disappear.

Blanca had asked Liguori to record everything that Marialuigia Moreno had written.

Early every morning, she sat down at her computer, put on her headphones with Neodymium speakers and soldered the sound to her ears.

The first time that she listened to the whole recording from start to finish she lingered, as she had on the other occasions, over the last few instants.

Liguori finished with a whisper of a voice, devoid of the tone of someone reading.

"There's darkness and then there's darkness."